THE CHRONICLES OF
PAISLEY · CORNERS

The longer you look at an object,
the more of the world you see in it.
— Flannery O'Connor

A NOVEL BY
CHERYL VAN DAALEN-SMITH, RN

FriesenPress

One Printers Way
Altona, MB R0G 0B0
Canada

www.friesenpress.com

This is a work of fiction. Names, characters, places and incidents either are products of the author's imagination or are used fictitiously.

This book is dedicated to Canada's Public Health Nurses with love.

ISBN
978-1-03-916290-7 (Hardcover)
978-1-03-916289-1 (Paperback)
978-1-03-916291-4 (eBook)

1. FICTION, HISTORICAL

Distributed to the trade by The Ingram Book Company

Dedication

To all the friends who supported this dream, helped me to keep going, read drafts, talked through characters, word choices, underlying messaging – thank you. To my husband for building me a writing hut, back in our little woods – thank you for this sanctuary. And to my little corgi Jack – whose been right there beside me for every single word. You are the best friend a girl could ever have.

Whether you're a nurse or someone who's been helped by a nurse, this is your chance to join 'Kick', a wise and devoted Public Health Nurse, to dive into how and why she cares for her real-life neighbours in rural Canada. A lovely, thoughtful, sharing of nursing's core values — stories Florence Nightingale would have loved!

–Deva-Marie Beck, PhD, RN, DTM
Barbara M. Dossey, PhD, RN, AHN-BC, FAAN, HWNC-BC
International Co-Directors of
the Nightingale Initiative for Global Health
https://www.NIGHvision.net

This gentle novel shines a spotlight on a Public Health Nurse's care for the people in a small rural community in Canada. The stories of the residents of *Paisley • Corners* are told with humour, warmth, and empathy and remind us of heartwarming relationships experienced in our own small communities.

–Melanie Whitfield & Barbara Pratt
The Lucy Maud Montgomery Society of Ontario.
https://lucymaudmontgomery.ca/

"…..van Daalen-Smith, an Ontario-based nurse, has crafted an engrossing narrative that conjures a world that combines the folksy appeal of Jan Karon's Mitford books with the nursing perspective and advocacy found in Jenny Worth's The Midwife (2009), the basis of a PBS series. van Daalen-Smith is particularly deft at capturing the angst of the tale's older characters and the town's political dynamics and moments of heartwarming charity…. This astute novel could be a springboard for a series."

– *Kirkus Reviews*

We all have a story and a context. We all crave connection. We all come from somewhere. And, in *Paisley • Corners* we can find "home". van-Daalen-Smith creates a kaleidoscopic view of human connection in rural community life and public health nursing practice. She impeccably knits a narrative of how and why history, context, and relationships matter.

The language in *Paisley • Corners* is so purposefully and power-fully chosen. The story line and character development are simply exquisite. Filled with eclectic characters, rich dialogue, and palpable settings, the story reads like soft paisley fabric, full of color, curves, and diverse patterns. The tone and tenor inspire the investments of kindness, empathy, and generous interpretations.

Paisley • Corners offers much comfort to any reader, but for nurses it is truly a special gem. The story is both relational and inspiring. The author seamlessly threads nursing metaparadigm, ethics and values, and the competencies a nurse requires to work with people in the comfort or messiness of their life's journey. Serving with grit and grace in equal measure, Nurse Kick models this beautifully. Nurse Kick's tailored approach is a testimony to the idea that nurses need be present, not perfect as we work with and for our clients. This book reminds us that within our client's story exists the antidote of bias and recipe for socially just and self-determined agency. For nurses, the story is a clear reminder of our why.

–Patricia M. King RN, MN
Community Health Nursing Instructor, University of Saskatchewan Provincial Representative and Member of the Standards and Competencies Committee of The Community Health Nurses of Canada

TABLE OF CONTENTS

PROLOGUE
PAISLEY · CORNERS, DOT INTENDED

Public health nurses are like the wind. While rarely seen, their presence is felt. They embed themselves deeply into a community, one interaction at a time, earning trust, affirming experiences, and assessing health. Present for hundreds of years, arriving to residences by foot, horse, carriage, and car, the PHN has provided quiet caring for generations of Canadians.

Paisley • Corners, a rural village north of Toronto, has had its share of PHNs. The last one retired a year ago, leaving quite the void—that is, until Kick Cavendish signed a contract and took it upon herself to fulfil her career dream of becoming a rural nurse. She longed for the quiet busyness of small towns and the promise of meaningful relationships for years with patients. She longed to work closely with the police, the mayor, the business owners, the churches. But most of all, Kick longed to make a difference. A real one. The kind that was subtly profound, eventually helping everyone believe that they mattered.

Sometimes a place is so beautiful that thoughts of its sumptuous trees, flowered hills, and endearing people float into your subconscious and tenderly strike root. Sometimes that place is so unsuspectedly impactful, you find yourself daydreaming about its lessons, wondering if you'd ever be able to explain how it feels to be there. That's the way it is for Public Health Nurse (PHN) Kick Cavendish when she thinks of her newly discovered Paisley • Corners (dot intended), especially at first light. Somehow, in the quiet of an imminent day, the sky, the wind, and the changing seasons appear all the more vivid. The rustic wonderland that is Paisley • Corners pulled her in. Together with her beloved Caleb—her high school sweetheart—she has set about to craft a new life; a life renewed, at least in part, by otherwise-forgotten farm animals and a new role as the village PHN.

Paisley • Corners isn't that different from other rural Ontario towns, what with its rich history, its founding families, and its battles over change, new stoplights, and who'll be in charge of the annual turkey supper. Maybe the dot in its name is a bit odd, but that's the way it's always been. Before the advent of postal codes and other ways of identifying addresses, the dot in Paisley • Corners' name signified its geographic relation to the broader community of Caledon. And even though it's no longer necessary, leaving the dot off of anything "official-like" will raise the ire of many a town citizen.

Nestled within the Niagara Escarpment and fed by the Headwaters of Dufferin County, Paisley • Corners, has in one way or another, been identifiable on Ontario maps since 1798. The first settlers arrived in the village in the early 1820s establishing essential services quickly. In its early halcyon days, Paisley • Corners boasted three hotels, a full-service general store, a livery stable, hat and harness makers, churches, an Orange Lodge, a creamery, and a beloved one-room schoolhouse at the top of the hill. A railway was built through the village in 1877, with a station house featuring the frugal design of a combined waiting room/freight room/station master's office typical of the times. Long since abandoned, the railway lands were claimed by a resolute committee, chaired (of course) by Mrs. Mabel Tarbox, to establish the Caledon Trailway: an ambling thirty-five kilometers of natural beauty, protected in perpetuity for hikers, cyclists, and horseback riders.

Before it came to be known as Paisley • Corners, this lovely spot had been called Tarbox Corners, Munsies' Corners, and a couple of other things. But no matter what it's been called, one thing has remained a constant: this place and its rural way of life gets in the blood of its inhabitants. To have your days organized by nature—by the hopeful planting times of spring, the buckle-down busyness of harvest time, and the wintertime all-hands-on-deck mentality that bubbles up when the main road becomes an ice rink—has an impact. This is even more true if you share your life with animals, and even truer yet if you're caring for a diverse group of rural dwellers who count on you every day. That's the way it is for Kick Cavendish, whose days are shaped partly by the weather, partly by the needs of her rescues, and partly by the sheer geography she's got to cover to make the day's community meetings and home visits. It's a lot to fit into a day, which is probably the reason why the animals she rescues tend to be minis: mini goats, mini horses, mini roosters. The smaller the rescue, the smaller the yield at mucking time.

Driving north out of the hamlet, Kick's rescue farm and little log home are at the bottom of the third hill— or is it the fourth? She still can't exactly remember, but tells people who ask that it's five minutes up the road from the 'Three and a Half' and to watch for the sign hanging in the trees at its entrance:

The *Three and a Half* is what everyone calls the center of town. Somehow, when the village was being built, the notion of four corners didn't materialize. So Paisley • Corners unapologetically boasts just three and a half corners. And all things Paisley • Corners seems to spring from the Three and a Half with pretty much everything being nearby.

Given all the goings on that Kick's come to learn about, one would think that the municipality of Paisley • Corners, population 2000, would be better known—like George Street in St. Johns, Newfoundland, or the waterfront area in Old Montreal. Nope. You scarcely know you've entered Paisley • Corners until you find yourself at the light. The *one* light. The first down-hill slope greets drivers with siding-faced houses, little yards, and various shops attached, haphazardly at times. A barbershop, a motorcycle repair, and a Sunday antique shop all appear, but only if you slow to take a longer look. The blend of old and new seems to work, at least for most. The respective efforts of the Paisley • Corners Historical Society and the Paisley • Corners Revitalization committee have made the Three and a Half a battleground of dreaming and remembering.

It's not as if the public health nurse knew *exactly* what she was going to do at this stage of her life, aside from wanting to live and work in rural Ontario. It's more that she *didn't* know. Kick didn't have a basement full of ducks and goats just waiting for her to discover an untenanted barn surrounded by twenty-five acres. But a longing to care for, protect and strengthen beings who were misunderstood and devalued had always been in the recesses of her heart—a longing both denied and met. Longings that, in part, brought her to a career in nursing. But it took Paisley • Corners and a vacant barn to re-open that space of her heart, long stymied by unspoken disappointments.

At first light, glimpses of connection between her animals, her patients, and the values that underpin public health nursing bring profound lessons that humble her, and eventually change her. For every day she travels along the long road from which Paisley • Corners stems, she is reminded, in an ever-deepening way, that health is a matter of who matters.

CHAPTER ONE
THE ARRIVAL OF KICK CAVENDISH

District Public Health Nurse Job Ad 20-12V

Responsibilities Include:

- Provide public health nursing assessment, treatment, education, counselling, consultation, referral, and advocacy;

- Coordinate and provide nursing care and community-development programs for/with individuals, families, groups, schools and community groups;

- Collaborate with community members, organizations, groups, families, and individuals with the objective of identifying the priorities of the community in order to promote the health of the population while addressing health and social inequities

If you are a self-starter who works well independently and within an interdisciplinary team, have a keen interest in rural nursing, we have the opportunity for you to make a real difference.

Must have a vehicle, have an earned BScN with a public health/ rural health focus and be registered 'in good standing' with the provincial regulatory body for Registered Nurses.

Please apply with resume, references, and a personal statement.

Road trips are better with dogs alongside, especially when you decide to take a chance and explore a new place. It was a November afternoon when Kick Cavendish drove back from her mother's final resting spot in the blue mountains of central Ontario. Hard to believe, she thought that four years had already passed since her mother's sudden and tragic passing. The drives home were always a mix of somber reflection and amber-lit contentment. When she was alive, Kick's mom had *always* kept on an amber light somewhere in her home, creating a warmth that seemed to soothe away even the most painful of heartaches. Beside Kick in the car was Petey, her Pembroke Welsh corgi, who contently sniffed the wet autumn air as they made their way back down the escarpment.

Her plan was to have a look around Paisley • Corners, now that she'd been hired to be the new public health nurse. She tried to keep her mind from drifting to sad thoughts or even joyful memories on these drives; although the route to Paisley • Corners was a direct one on a single road, the drive was known to be dangerous. Suddenly, out of the corner of her eye, Kick saw a sign way high up on a tree:

Log Home for Sale

And then it was gone. Still driving, she let it register. After a slight hesitation, rooted solely in the assumption that housing in this area of Ontario would be far out of her and Caleb's reach, she turned her jeep around and announced to her Corgi companion, "Why not? ... Let's go have a look."

And in *that* very moment, the life she'd known began to change. Turning the jeep around was an unconsidered decision: one that allowed the easily-missed hamlet of Paisley • Corners to render itself visible.

Down the long and windy driveway they went, past an empty paddock on their left and a wonderful Christmas tree-lined hill on the right. Suddenly, there in front of them was a weathered board and batten barn with a red tin roof, two sets of double-Dutch doors, five stalls, and a recently swept concrete floor.

Serendipitously in front of Kick Cavendish was the barn of her longing—an unconscious yearning birthed at that precise and innocent moment. Somehow, on some level, she understood that this red-roofed barn, enveloped by this little rural hamlet, was an opportunity. For what, she was not sure. Sometimes thunder comes *before* the light.

As she and Petey began to explore, wondering if there was any chance this spot could somehow become theirs, she spotted a disheveled man with a kindly face quickly walking up a path out back of the house. She called out, "Hello there."

He stopped and waved meekly. She thought to herself that he had kind eyes and seemed a bit afraid. His face was weather beaten, as were his hands, and when they shook hello, for a fleeting moment, he reminded her of someone. To her, he seemed like that safe and gentle neighborhood grandpa you knew when you were a child. "Do you live here?" she asked the kindly man, sensing his unease and intentionally holding his hand gently.

"Uh, no, no. I'm just checkin' on the place is all," he replied, glancing up the path repeatedly. He reached down to pet the little corgi, who'd planted himself at the man's feet.

"I don't want to keep you. I'm Kick Cavendish and I'm the new public health nurse. I hope it's okay that we have a look around. The sign says this place is for sale, and so I thought I'd take a chance and drive in to have a look."

The man gave a single nod to which Kick answered appreciatively with her eyes. She's met men like him before, she thought. Longing to connect but ashamed of their diminished essence. In that moment, as automatic as breathing, his dignity pushed out any thoughts she'd had of exploring this house, this barn, this property. A human was in front of her, and right now he deserved her full attention.

As she was about to shift the conversation to the weather, the trees and the gentleman, he turned his shoulders, preparing to depart. Kick reached out her hand and touched his shoulder. "It sure was nice to meet you," she said.

With half a smile, he raised his eyes, momentarily meeting hers for the first time. It was a gentle moment—one of many experienced humbly, appreciatively, by nurses on the job, and one foreshadowing the many moments of humble connection awaiting Kick in her imminent role as the rural hamlet's PHN.

Before she knew it, the man was gone, leaving subtle contentment to linger in her nurse's soul.

Pausing to take in the beauty of her surroundings, Kick sat down on one of the huge rocks on the edge of the pond behind the house. "Petey, do you think there's even a slight chance this might be where we can move to?" Petey drank from the portable pet dish she (always) had in her purse, contently laying his head on the moist grass beside the rock. With a medley of trees in front of her including sumac, birch, oak, maple, beech and ash, Kick found herself relaxing.

Her smile was interrupted with the stark realization that they'd probably been there far too long! After all, it *was* private property. She gathered up her belongings, scratched Petey on the forehead, and made her way back to the front of the house. Looking up at the trees in the middle of the circular driveway and the cayenne-red roof of both the house and the barn, she started to hope—just a little.

It didn't take too many months for Kick and her husband Caleb to sign the papers and move into the hamlet of Paisley • Corners. At the same time, she prepared to pursue her other more conscious dream to be a rural public health nurse and focused in on all the orientation documents required for the position. "The stars have lined up for you," her father had told her, back when she told him of the opening and of her successful interview for the position of PHN of Paisley • Corners.

In the three months between her discovery of this sweet village and their February moving day, she'd been thinking a lot about the healing energies of animals: something she'd witnessed as a public health nurse working with persons affected by trauma. She had discovered that alpacas have a vibrational energy that is calming and grounding. Like dolphins, alpacas have been known to possess gentle energies that quell the stirrings of longings unmet—at least, they did for Kick and Caleb. And so, in their first year in Paisley • Corners, Kick went to an alpaca show at the local fairgrounds.

Unsure of just what to expect, she found herself overwhelmed with not only the visual beauty of these gentle creatures, but also of their calm and inquisitive natures. Out back of the main show ring, owners of various alpacas had separate stalls where they kept their animals. There is where Kick set herself down beside a pen of five Alpacas, two moms and their three *crias*. She found a chair and pulled up beside them, speaking ever so quietly… all the while feeling their pull—feeling their draw.

"You seem lost in thought, young lady," said a rail-thin man with a scraggly beard. With a wry smile on his face and a beat-up John Deere cap on his head, he introduced himself to her. "Delbert White's the name, and those are our alpacas. You like?"

"Oh my, yes. They're so ... well ... beautiful. I can't stop looking at them. Their eyes look as though they're filled with liquid. And the babies are so trusting and inquisitive. I don't know what it is ... I just feel calm and at ease sitting here. I love them so much."

"Do you have any of your own?" he asked, starting to unlock the pen.

"Oh no, but I'd just love to have some. I wouldn't even know where to start!"

"Here, I'll put one of the Crias on a lead and you can exercise him a bit." And so Delbert White handed Kick the lead, and almost at the same moment, she felt her heart swell with love. As Kick started to lead the baby out to the exercise area, Delbert's wife Ellie came and smiled at her, saying, "I see Delbert came to talk to you, eh? He's been watching you all morning—telling me that he thought he could see you slowly falling in love."

"He's right about that," Kick answered. "I'm Kick. Kick Cavendish. Pleased to meet you, Ellie."

"We're just about to have lunch over yonder by the registration tables. Care to join us?"

"Oh yes, that would be lovely."

She handed the lead back to Delbert and whispered to the Cria, "There you go little one. Back to your mom."

The three had lunch together, minestrone soup and half a veggie wrap for Kick, tomato soup and cheese sandwiches for the Whites. Kick asked them about their lives with alpacas, how they got started, and all that was involved in caring for them. And before she knew it, they'd invited her to their farm in Beaverton, Ontario to see what they did and to pick her own alpacas, if she was serious about getting some. She *was* serious—and she was scared. *What if I don't know how to do it?* she worried. *What if I can't give them a good life?* Kick would often worry about these sorts of things—about if she could give animals or people the life they deserved—a life in which they knew that they mattered and were loved. Into Kick and Caleb's life came Casper, the sweetest albino alpaca, whose herd had rejected him, forcing his owner to keep Casper in a separate pen alone. Along with Casper came Michael, a shy black alpaca with alopecia. What a pair! Later, Kick would add two other sweet brown males, making a fine-looking foursome.

Her fortuitous trip to the alpaca show gave rise to the eventual formation of a small but loving rescue farm of cast-away animals who would now know only love and predictability.

Little did Kick and Caleb know that many things they'd see in their barn would be so instructive for their own lives, mirroring human experiences and illuminating important values.

CHAPTER TWO
OLD JOE

All of them wore the cast-off clothes of other men and women, were made up of patches and pieces of other people's individuality and had no sartorial existence of their own proper.
"Little Dorrit" Charles Dickens - 1855

Every small town has one: a guy everyone thinks they know without ever taking the time to do so. The guy everyone thinks they're different from—better than. The guy who gets blamed for his circumstances and for all his supposed character flaws. The guy who, for most, could never fit the local definition of normal or proper or good enough. The guy who, when spotted, becomes the day's local gossip. The guy who never ever looks up when he's walking, and who, despite his advancing years, walks briskly and discreetly, determined to not be noticed. This is the kind of person that Canada's Public Health nurses advocate for, partner with, and care about.

Oh sure, big cities probably have hundreds of these nameless fellas, rendered inconspicuous by shame or reproach, but small towns like Paisley • Corners usually have just one or two. Georgetown, a larger town than Paisley • Corners and not too far away, has the "Chicken Man," who rides his bike with a red milk crate fastened over the back wheel, within which his beloved hen can always be found. Harrowsmith has the "Coin Lady," who can be seen scouring the neighborhood for small change and then using it to pay her bill at the local Cheese Factory. Penetanguishene had "Pop Bottle Percy," who, when pop bottles were plenty, searched for and collected enough to pay cash for his second-hand Buick LeSabre. And Paisley • Corners has Old Joe, of no fixed address—except for P.O. Box 1, Paisley • Corners, Ontario. And he *does* have himself a post office box. Just ask Paisley • Corners' substitute postmistress, Dotty Pinkney. She'll tell you, "He comes in the last Friday of every month just like clockwork, stinking to high heaven and smiling just the same."

It didn't take too long for Kick to learn that nearly *everyone* here in Paisley • Corners thinks he's odd, especially after Old Joe wrote the local paper that he was happy when Foodville went twenty-four hours—and to please keep it that way. Now he could shop when no one else did, when young Tanis Eccles was on cash in the middle of the night. Tanis was paying her way through nursing school and could typically be found engrossed in a pile of anatomy and physiology books, studying for one exam or another. Joe convinced himself she didn't notice his dirty fingernails, or the fermented Aqua Velva he'd apply on shopping days.

Years back, before he could go into Foodville in the middle of the night, Joe would go in on Tuesday nights around six-thirty, when Loretta Putney was finishing her one and only weekly shift—the one time during the week when she was able to do her own thing and have a break from her beloved Ambrose. When she was alive, Loretta *always* treated Old Joe well. Happy to see him, signaled by a gentle hand on his stained and faded Bay coat, Loretta might've been the one person he would talk to about his life, if he ever became so inclined.

But don't hold your breath about Joe ever talking about anything to *any*one. You see, not everyone in Paisley • Corners is like Miss Loretta. Not everyone thinks that Old Joe is even worth a passing mention in conversation, except for some who think he simply needs to go. Around the time Kick arrived, Old Joe had been the center of many a conversation. In fact, Old Joe had been the third agenda item for a month now in the meetings of the local Revitalization Committee. Some members wanted to invite the commander of the Paisley • Corners Ontario Provincial Police detachment, Theodore Bucket, to a meeting to talk about how to get Old Joe to leave. And even many of the long-standing members of the Paisley • Corners Historical Society had been talking about him, with tonight's meeting being no exception.

Along with Old Joe, the hamlet's new PHN found herself on the agenda as well, providing an opportunity to discuss her role and to introduce herself.

"Can everyone please take their seats? We'll be starting shortly," Mabel Tarbox announced, gently placing a hand on the backs of any remaining tea table stragglers. The warmth of Mabel Tarbox's gentle, guiding hands is an experience nearly everyone in Paisley • Corners can claim. A gentle hand on the back is the approach she's used to organize people for decades. Whether it be children just in from recess at the PC public school, ladies at a Presbyterian Church Women meeting, or at any number of local committees she's chaired over the years, Mabel Tarbox has made sure anything she was involved in was respectful of the participants *and* went smoothly. A planner, she was. Is.

Tonight's meeting was no different, even if it was being held in her kitchen. Mabel lives right smack in the centre of the hamlet, steps from the church, the townhall, the post office, and the hair salon.

And Mabel likes it that way. Her modest house has a screened-in porch that she never locks. On any given day, you find things left there for her or things she's left for someone to come and pick up, like the keep-warm bags for when she delivers for *Meals on Wheels*.

Today, she'd spent the better part of an hour cleaning her already-tidy kitchen so that it would be ready for the meeting this evening. She'd watered her garden out front and all of her house plants were placed just so on the kitchen windowsills. Just in case, she'd dusted the parlor and smoothed the lace doilies that adorn her two sitting chairs and her olive-green loveseat.

At tonight's PC Historical Society meeting, Mabel made sure everyone signed in, has their name tag on, and has an agenda. For her, a meeting is good when the tea is hot, the milk is cold and things begin on time.

As Mabel made her way around her kitchen, doling out nametags, a newcomer approached her. "Excuse me—uh, I'm Mrs. Tarbox, and you are?"

"I'm Kick Cavendish, the new …"

"Oh yes, our new nurse. Well. I've made you a name tag, Mrs. Cavendish, and …"

"Please call me Kick. Everyone does."

"Uh, yes, well, uh, Kick. How … unique! Please put your nametag on and help yourself to some tea. We're glad to welcome you here, and I'll let you know when it's your turn to speak."

Kick thanked her and wandered off to find a chair. Mabel found her seat at the head of the kitchen table, and Dotty Pinkey sat beside her as usual. As secretary, Dotty Pinkney always makes sure that something historical about Paisley • Corners is on the agenda every meeting. Nothing is more important to her than preserving history – always taking pictures and labeling them.

"I would like to call this meeting to order," announced Mabel, attempting to be heard over the chatter.

11

But before Mabel has a chance to officially begin the meeting, Dotty interjected. "He's an eye sore, and he smells something awful," she said, scrunching her nose and waving her hand in front of it.

Eyes blinking in disbelief, Mabel turned her head to look at the Society secretary. "Lands sake, Dotty. Must you go on and on like this? Will you let me start the meeting? We're not even at that agenda item. We need to go back to our agenda and stick with it. You should know that, Dotty," urged Mabel, looking uncharacteristically exasperated. "After all, you *are* the secretary of the Paisley • Corners Historical Society, are you not?"

Mabel, normally tolerant and even keeled, had grown increasingly impatient with Dotty's focus on Old Joe. Similar to the agenda of the PC Revitalization Committee, Item Three of tonight's Historical Society meeting was also Old Joe, but for *very* different reasons.

"We're only on the first agenda item: minutes of the previous meeting," declared Mabel. "We can talk about Old Joe when we get to that item on the agenda."

And with that, the room erupted in side-conversations about Dotty, Joe, and the battle that had been brewing between the Paisley • Corners Historical Society and the Paisley • Corners Revitalization Committee.

"I can't help it, is all," Dotty declared. "He is an eye sore, and I agree with that new committee, whatever they're calling themselves—but mark my words, this will be the *only* thing I'll ever agree with them about."

"Order, order!" Mabel requested, tapping her oak gavel.

Mabel Tarbox has been the president of the Historical Society for as long as anyone can remember. And Dotty Pinkney has long been the secretary, the treasurer, or both. It depends. Dotty's availability is always contingent upon whether she is needed to fill in at the post office. "Ooh, it depends," she'll say, when asked what days might be good for the next meeting. "Mary Offenbach isn't getting any younger and I have to be at the ready in case she needs me to take a shift or two."

"Okay," Mabel stated after everyone has quieted down, "Let's have a review of our previous meetings minutes. Dotty, could you please review the minutes for us?"

Dotty dutifully obliged. "Minutes of the Paisley • Corners Historical Society. President Mabel Tarbox welcomed members and guests to our fall harvest themed meeting. Agnes Wright of the Caledon Horticultural Society gave a presentation on the history of lost apple crops, discussing how warm Marches and April snowstorms have blighted many the apple crops through history. Members enjoyed coffee and conversation while viewing Dot Pinkney's photo display of all things Paisley • Corners. The meeting wrapped up at eight-thirty p.m."

"Any errors or omissions?" asked Mabel Tarbox. "Hearing none, I move approval of these minutes. All in favour?" Everyone raised his or her hands. Well, nearly everyone.

One person did not: Goody Flannigan, Paisley • Corners Elementary School's colourful principal.

On any given day, you'll see Goody working as not only the principal, but the crossing guard, lunch lady, and custodian. She has a distinct key for every role—fifteen, to be exact, and all hanging from the same keychain appended to the same belt. Didn't matter what she was wearing—pants, a dress, a skirt—no diff. Same belt. Same key chain. Same characteristic jingle as it rhythmically bounces off her ample hip. Oh, and in her spare time, she's now owner of the new consignment store, *Goody's*, on the northwest corner of the hamlet's center.

She wasn't pleased that the minutes failed to mention the gall of the PC Revitalization Committee setting up a posterboard display at the last Historical Society's meeting, outlining their plan to "beautify" Paisley • Corners. But uncharacteristically, Goody Flannigan held her tongue. She was, after all, *finally* on tonight's agenda, so she waited and stewed.

"Okay," Mabel continued, "Thank you, Dotty. Now. Business arising. Item Number One. We need to talk about the plan to erect a mural downtown. Goody," Mabel smiled, "this is your agenda item, so I'll hand the discussion over to you."

"Thank you very much, Miss Mabel," Goody began. "You all remember that ghastly poster do-hickey dem newcomers put up at our last meeting, doncha? 'Beautify' Paisley • Corners. Hmmfff. The nerve. I for one am against it."

"As background for anyone who wasn't at our last meeting," Mabel interjected, "I'll just mention that the Historical Society has been asked in a formal letter by the Revitalization Committee to approve their plan for a mural in downtown Paisley • Corners. They wish to place it on the wall of the old fire hall, as it'll depict the old fire wagon, the FireEttes, and the new fire truck. Is there any discussion?" asked Mabel. "The chair recognizes Josephine Fraser."

"I'd prefer if you'd call me Jo," requested Jo Fraser, a retired outpost nurse. "I think it's a great idea. I don't see the problem with putting murals up, as long as they show some of the old and some of the new. I think it's time has come. I welcome it. The fact that they are asking us is a good thing. It shows that they respect us and our committee's mandate."

"Thank you Jo, for your comments," replied Mabel. "Other comments?"

"Bet you wouldn't be saying this if it was in Cheltenham," challenged Dotty. "What if they wanted to deface the Cheltenham General Store with a mural? What would you think of that, Miss Josephine Jo Fraser?"

To that, Jo Fraser smiled and replied, "I realize, Dotty, I haven't been here as long as you or your kinfolk, but if it were to happen in Cheltenham, I'd also welcome it."

Meanwhile, Olive Patterson was waving her hand in the back of the room. Mabel nodded at her. "The chair recognizes Olive Patterson. Olive, please go ahead," Mabel said.

"My daughter knows somebody who's a painter. We could have that person paint it," offered Olive.

"Well ... " Mabel cautiously responded, " Olive, I know you really would like to get your daughter back involved in things here, but it seems to me that the Paisley • Corners Arts Council have their own painters that are going to do it, and I think they're only really coming to us to ask what we think of the plan and whether we could support it. Thank you so much, though, for this offer. I'll tell them this in case they need anyone."

Mabel has always treated Olive with respect and dignity, unlike others who simply have "no time" to wait for Olive to say what she wants to say or remember what she was going to say. Mabel conducts herself and anything she is involved in with decorum. "Now Olive, do you have any thoughts about their plan?" she asked.

"Oh no, no, it sounds okay to me. I have no problem with it. I just thought my daughter ... my daughter, you know ... she lives up north now. She has her own farm. Do you know that? She has her own farm. Sheep. And oh, the wool. This year she's working on new shades of green. That's in now, it's simply all the rage," Olive continued.

"Oh, there she goes again," mumbled Dotty Pinkney, rolling her eyes. "She just goes off on these tangents, and I don't know."

"Shhhh," Jo Fraser whispered, elbowing Dotty. "Stop being so negative. Why do you have to be so negative?"

Shuffling in their seats, some of the ladies put their sweaters on. Others got up to refresh their tea. Kick wasn't exactly sure what was going on, so she opted to stay silent and listen.

"Order, order!" demanded Mabel, tapping the gavel. She got up to close the porch door, as the evening's air had begun to come in. "Can we please return to the agenda? I see you, Goody. You might as well go ahead, as I don't see any other hands up, so we can end with your final comments."

"I's swear if I see just one of these chuckleheads, I'll be askin' dem if dey were born on a raft. Just who do dese city folk tink dey are, suggesting we needs *beautifyin*? Just look at our forests, our roadside flowers, our skies, our farms, and lilacs, and some of Canada's most stunnin' horses. I hears tell of a confounded yoga studio. Yoga! Next, we'll be havin' one of dose internet fancy coffee outfits where's dey all smoke the wacky tobacky and kick off deir socks and sandals and have free sex. Dey calls it *hookin up*," bleared Goody. "Deys want to tear down de old Orange Hall building and build demselves a building with solar doo whatchamacallits. Der stund as me arse, I's tell ya."

Whenever Goody gets her ire up, you can hear the Newfoundland in her. From Big Pond, she is. Home is never far from her heart, or any other Newfoundlander, that's for sure. Aside from when she gets on the phone with her son and grandkids back in Clarenville, the only other time you'll hear her style of speech shift so emphatically is when she and Gus at the gas station get talkin' about back home. She'll tell Gus he just *has* to go to her son Stephen's pub. "It's easy to find, I tells ya. Flannigan's Pub's right der in Clarenville. My Henry, God rest 'is soul, used'a run it a ways back whens we were just young. He liked da bottle, I tells ya. Pretty nears killed 'im. Da bottle, dat is. Not da pub. And now's my son runs it and ooo eee, da fish is fresher 'dan any udder pub, you's can be sure as 'dat!" Goody would proclaim.

"Well, Goody, we certainly understand your view on all of this. Any other discussion?" asked Mabel, attempting to take back control of the meeting. She paused and waited. "Seeing none, I'm going to put forth the vote. All in favour of the Paisley • Corners Arts Council's request that they put up a mural?"

"—and that's it?" added Dotty.

"Dotty, you can't add that. You can't add 'that's it,'" corrected Mabel. "All in favour? Opposed? Abstentions?" she asked.

"Ab what?" asked Goody.

"Ab. Sten. Shuns. It means you are neither here nor there on a given issue. Or it signals that you have a conflict of interest and so withhold any vote," replied Mabel.

"Oh, this high-falutin jibber jabber. Dees types got brains as scarce as hen's teeth. Let's get on" demanded Goody.

"Ok, then, any abstentions?" asked Mabel. "Well, it seems as if we do not have a clear direction on this. Hmmm … Not sure just what we should do. We need to get back to them with an answer about the mural question."

But the subject of Old Joe was already pulling attention away from the mural. "They want to get rid of Old Joe. If we give them this, they'll think we agree with their ways … that we agree Paisley • Corners needs changing. Needs improvement," said Jo, shaking her head.

Just then, out of the corner of her eye, Mabel saw a woman enter her kitchen through the screen door of the back porch. She didn't know this woman, who had the loveliest long eyelashes, straight black hair, meticulous make-up, and a canary-yellow, long silk dress with matching silk pants. Her hands were decorated all over with ornamental shapes in reddish, inky lines, off set only by a beautiful diamond with a matching diamond band, set in platinum, adorning her left hand.

The entire meeting of the Paisley • Corners Historical Society turned to look at her. "Oh my, sorry. I was trying to get here earlier and enter without disrupting your meeting; I was waiting outside for an opportune moment," the mysterious woman explained.

"Welcome," said Mabel, attempting to hide how startled she was by the beautiful stranger. "Please join us and let us know who you are."

"Thank you very much. I'm Sinny Bhattacherjee-Smythe," the stranger announced in an alto voice with a posh British accent. "I know I'm new to your lovely town, and I realize that perhaps I shouldn't have any input on the matter of the mural because of that, but I would really welcome some colour downtown. It's already beautiful there—well, here—but I believe it could use a splash more. I believe a mural would be a great idea. I for one, would be in favour of it, and I might be able to help consult with the Revitalization

Committee on its contents in a few months, once I attend to a few things," said Sinny.

"Thank you, Mrs. Smythe, for that input," Mabel replied. "I hope you come back to all of our meetings. And when you do, be sure you get yourself a nametag until I can order you a proper one."

"Let's move on to our next agenda item: choosing a speaker for our annual Spring Meeting. I understand someone had an idea. Who was it?" said Mabel, thumbing through her notes. "Ginger, I believe it was you."

Ginger Hogan is the local hairdresser who tries to know something about everyone. Oh, not in a negative way, but moreso in a conversational way. Folks have been coming to see her for decades, many just for the time she spends listening to them talk about their lives. She's got a lot to say too, mostly about her family and her big burly husband. Looking around at her fellow Historical Society members, Ginger Hogan cleared her throat. "Well, I was thinking that we could have the history of hairstyles in Paisley • Corners. You know, I've been doing hair here for near thirty years, and I could present all the changes in hairstyles over the years ... and the changes in products ... I could tell you the things that have happened at the salon," she offered excitedly.

"Ugh," mumbled Dotty, "she goes on and on about the hairdressing stuff all the blasted time."

"Shhhhhh," urged Jo again, elbowing Dotty harder this time. "Dotty, why do you have to always be so critical ... about everything?" Then Jo put up her hand.

Mabel nodded at her. "The chair recognizes Josephine—no, Jo— yes, Jo Fraser. Sorry, Jo. Go ahead."

"Thank you, Mabel. I appreciate it. I think we should have that guy come in to talk about the history of concessions in Caledon, especially with all the newcomers arriving. They mayn't know a concession from a rural road, a line, a side road, or a highway. I think it'd be interesting and bring with it a good deal of our history, too."

"Trut is, dey don't know der arse from a crawfish," laughed Goody.

"I'd love to hear about that history again, and I could most certainly arrange it," said Jo first nodding at Goody and then looking back in the direction of the chairwoman.

"Thank you, Jo. Any other ideas?"

"Wasn't Mr. Munsie Sr. going to come and do a history of Munsie's Feed and Farm supply?" asked Olive.

"Oh, yes," Mabel replied, "That is correct. Now, when was that scheduled for? Let me see, let me see ... Oh, here it is. I believe we said it would be best in the fall. Yes. Okay, let's vote. All those who want the History of Caledon Concessions, raise your hands ... And those in favour of us first going with the history of Munsie's Feed and Farm Supply? —Uh, Olive, you, uh, you can't vote twice dear," said Mabel, smiling gently.

"Oh, did I? Silly me. Well, honestly, I like the idea about the hairstyles we've had in Paisley • Corners. I remember when I had a bob. Oh my, it was all the rage back then. And my hair was thick and shiny and ..."

"Olive, Olive. Sorry, I'm just aware of the time, and of the tea getting cold," interrupted Mabel with as much gentleness as she could muster. "Ok ... So it appears the votes lean towards the concession and rural road topic first, and then next fall, we'll go with the Munsie's topic."

Olive's eyes dropped, feeling dejected.

"Good," Mabel continued, "Now, let's move onto Agenda Item Three, and that is how the Paisley • Corners Revitalization Committee wants to address the presence of Old Joe."

"Lard tunderin' Jesus. Finally! Waitin around for tings, a person could grow a nudder set of ..."

"Okay," interrupted Jo Fraser, trying to keep Goody from getting into her colourful language in front of the new guest.

"I'm telling you," announced Dotty, "that we need to do something about him. I'm telling you, we're getting all these sorts of

high-browed lawyer types and business types moving in. I even heard
that one of them wants to build a helicopter pad and runway. The guy
owns his own company, don't ya know, and wants to fly to and from
his work in the city!" Of course, Dot hadn't *heard* this; she *read* it
just last week at the post office. "Personally, I don't think that should
be allowed, and second of all, these well-to-do city professionals are
coming in here and we've got this smelly, wrinkled hobo coming into
the post office every Friday like clockwork, don't I know, and then to
the grocery store, and what if he goes to the hair salon one day when
one of the new ones are there?"

With a slight furled brow, Jo piped up, "I don't follow you, Dot.
You seem to be arguing both sides of the debate."

"I don't see any problem with him getting his mail, or getting
groceries, or getting his hair done," exploded Olive. "I don't know
what your problem is. I don't know why you always have to say such
derogatory things about Old Joe. He's harmless, I'm telling you, and
if I had my way, I'd help him every day, in any way I could."

"I completely agree," added Jo. "I don't know what it is people
have against this gentleman. He's harmless, yes, but more than that,
he's getting older just like many of us. We really should be looking out
for him, helping him, and welcoming him once and for all. I worry
when I don't hear that someone has spotted him, even though they're
usually gossiping. I think it is our job to help him and he is part of our
history. We *are* the Historical Society, are we not?"

"He's never come into the hair salon," remarked Ginger, "but I'd
have no problem cutting his hair. Lord knows he needs it. But I'd have
to disinfect my combs after."

"Excuse me, ladies, but I have a question, if I might."

"The chair recognizes Mrs. Smythe."

"Thank you so very much, Madame Chair." Sinny smiled. "Thank
you. I have a question and that is who exactly is this 'Old Joe?' Can
someone tell me who this person is and what all the trouble is about?"

"I will," said Olive Patterson.

"The chair recog—"

"Oh for God's sake, will ya' just let a body speak? Lard Tunderin!" burst Goody.

Olive slowly stood up, cupping the fingers of one hand in the other, and prepared to explain the whole thing. "Old Joe is a person who has lived in Paisley • Corners for decades and decades. I've lived in Paisley • Corners for decades and decades, too. We used to raise Clydesdales. My Jim was known all over Canada for his Clydesdales. We have diplomas and certificates in boxes that fill our crawl space. This was when I was raising my girls ..."

"Olive dear," Mabel interrupted, "come on back. Let's tell Mrs. Smythe about Old Joe, shall we?" asked Mabel.

Everyone has heard that Olive has been diagnosed with early Alzheimer's, but it is Mabel who usually tries the hardest to help Olive find her thoughts and make her point.

Olive blinked. "Right, Old Joe. As I was saying, he's lived in Paisley • Corners for years and years and years, although we don't know exactly where he lives ..."

"He's of no fixed address," Dotty added snidely. "He's N. F. Aaaaa! And gracious providence, I know this because he has a post office box and ..."

"Dotty, please wait your turn," Mabel asserted. "Olive, go on please."

"Joe is a kindly older gentleman who wouldn't hurt anybody. And you barely ever see him. And when you do, he's got his head down, just trying to get out of people's sight. It's sad, really. We're all responsible for that—for him feeling ashamed just to walk around in Paisley • Corners. I see no harm in him and I find it deeply offensive, what people say. Everybody has a story, that's what I know. And who knows through what series of events Joe ended up here with us, down and out. Everybody has a story. Everybody has reasons that they end up in the circumstances that others so easily judge from the outside. And it is not for us to judge at all."

21

"Yes; 'cast ye the first stone,'" added Mabel Tarbox, staring off in the distance. "'He who is without sin, cast ye the first stone.'" Mabel often liked to quote scripture.

Now that Olive was warmed up, she had a few more thoughts to share on the matter. "You know, I don't even know if any of this is even about sin, as some would like to imply. What I think is sinful, to be honest, is this judgment of people who are calling themselves a *revitalization committee* suggesting that a human being is something to be rid of ... that in order for a hamlet such as ours to be revitalized so to speak, it needs to clear out the supposed derelicts. I'm offended by it. And I, for one, believe that our committee should write a stern letter to them. They are trying to change everything. The offensiveness of having a *person*, a human being who loves, longs, grieves, and bleeds just the same as anyone else, of making them an agenda item to *address* is completely and utterly unacceptable. How dare they?" And with that, Olive Patterson smoothed her skirt, tilted her head, as if to implore all to see the indignity of the matter, and sat back down.

Olive Patterson would often have these returning moments of brilliance ... of showing her bright mind and clear articulation of complex issues. And in that monologue in the front room of the Historical Society's president, everyone—including Olive—saw a glimmer of what once was so effortless now receding as her mind slowly clouds over. As the thought of this looming and permanent loss took over, Olive became quite silent, and didn't speak for the remainder of the meeting.

"Hmm, I see. Why doesn't this man go to Toronto, where there are more services for people like that? Can't he go to Toronto? Surely there's much more there for him, in terms of supports and programs" asked Sinny.

In the back of the room, Kick Cavendish quietly raised her hand. She realized she must've been forgotten, but didn't want to interrupt the discussion. The Society remained too absorbed in discussion to see her upraised hand.

"Why should he have to go to Toronto?" asked Jo Fraser. "And, no offence to your suggestion, Mrs. Smythe, but who are we, as residents of Paisley • Corners, to say who should live here and who should not? It's not like Old Joe is causing problems. It's not like he's doing anything negative. I remember that Loretta Putney used to say before she died, that she thought there was lot more to him than any of us ever realized. And when I asked her about it, she said she'd rather just leave it at that. Loretta's husband Ambrose would often be gone for hours at a time. She became convinced that he was usually off looking for Old Joe, and that they'd spend whole days together fishing or something. Lorretta told me, 'He'd always come back without his coat or sweater.' She figured that Ambrose had given whatever it was to Old Joe. Once, she told me, he came back without his shoes and when pressed, he shrugged his shoulders and promised he'd go look for them the next again day. I think that was the same day she told me Ambrose came home covered in red dirt … dirt all in his socks, and all over his head and hands. And on the back of his white baseball hat, he'd had red sand. When she asked him about it, he would again shrug, even though they both knew he had made it all the way over to the badlands in Cheltenham. And this was no easy feat … especially without shoes! But anyway, I agree with Olive, that we should be writing a stern letter and sending it off."

After a moment of silence, Mabel took the reigns again. "Alright then. I think we've had quite a good amount of discussion this evening. It's time we have our tea, and I believe Ginger's made her famous gingersnap cookies."

"I surely did. Yes siree. Just before we went up to the trailer," answered Ginger.

"So, just before this meeting is adjourned, who offers to draft up this letter?" asked Mabel.

"I will!" Olive offered.

"Dotty, can you help with that?" asked Mabel.

"Oh, I don't know … I'm really quite busy with the post office, covering shifts. I have to be ready at a moment's notice, just in case they need me," replied Dotty hesitatingly.

"Oh all right, I'll help too, if you wish," added Jo. She's used to jumping in when no one else wanted to—an old habit from her days as an outpost nurse on the prairies.

"Just don't be putting my name on that letter. I don't agree with it!" added Dotty, retrieving the tea kettle she'd left set to low.

"Any other business? None, then?" Mabel leaned back in her chair. "Alright, well, a big thanks to Ginger for tea and snacks, a big welcome to Mrs. Smythe for coming, and next time for snacks, it'll be Jo."

"I'd be pleased. I'll bring some of my preserves," replied Jo as she put on her alpaca yarn sweater.

With that, Kick stood up, brought her hands to her heart, and hurriedly stated, "I really want to thank you all for inviting me to your meeting. I'm Kick Cavendish, the new public health nurse. You've possibly seen me around town for a bit. I've met some of you already," she said, discretely smiling at Olive and Goody, "and I look forward to learning more about your hamlet, and what is important to you. If I might be of any help, I'd appreciate the chance to contribute. If Joe—er, Mister … sorry, I didn't catch his last name—might benefit from a home visit, that is something I can certainly do. I can link him with many resources he may not know about. Of course, it would be up to him. I've left my cards on the tea table. They include my cell phone number, as well as the number of the health department."

"Oh my!" Mabel replied. "I'm so sorry we didn't get to you Mrs. Caven—ah, Kick. Would you be able to come back to another meeting and talk a bit more about yourself and what you do?"

"It would be my pleasure. Thank you."

As Kick drove home, up the main artery of the hamlet from which most of its history has sprung, she reflected on her years as a street nurse, and the hundreds of Old Joes desperately in need of support, yet resistant to accepting it. What she heard tonight at the meeting wasn't new or unique: manifestations of marginalization, victim-blaming, and hierarchy occur everywhere, regardless of geography. How could she be of assistance without losing the trust of the village, which she'd yet to earn? Would Joe want to sit with her, talk to her? Was it her place to change the views of her newly appointed population? She set her mind to planting seeds. This strategy for change has been enacted by many a cautious public health nurse.

Kick pulled into her driveway shifting her thoughts to putting her rescues to bed for the night.

The next Monday, Kick read over the referrals and appointments for the day. She had an early meeting with her preceptor to close things off and give her a wee gift for orienting her when she first arrived. Then she was off to see Mr. Abner Wilkes, of Finnerty Sideroad, for a cardiovascular follow-up visit subsequent to his diagnosis of TIAs. She knew she had her work cut out for her, convincing him to heed the warnings of these mini strokes.

Still, "Old Joe" weighed heavily on her mind. She was sorry to conclude that it seemed as though almost everyone she'd met in Paisley • Corners had an opinion of Old Joe. Dotty Pinkney thinks he smells, Mabel Tarbox feels sorry for him, and Bob the septic guy calls him "a low-life, good-fer-nuthin." Malcolm Putney cautions his brother Ambrose not to go looking for Joe. Secretly, Ambrose doesn't always listen. Olive Patterson leaves her husband's hand-me-down jackets or sweaters in strategic places all around Paisley • Corners, hoping Old Joe might happen by. "I hate the thought of him being cold," she tells the grocery store clerk, or Mabel, or, well, anyone. And Josephine Fraser, who asks everyone to call her "Jo," has always wished she could find out where Joe lived so she "could help him out, just a bit."

Of all the people who think poorly of Old Joe, it's Abner Wilkes who hates him most. And not because he's an eyesore or anything like that. It's because Abner knows what everyone else doesn't: Old Joe is a good person. A kind person. Abner knows he spends much of his time helping the various residents of Paisley • Corners behind the scenes. City folks call it *random acts of kindness*. Old Joe would probably call it, "Just doin' my part." For Abner, this "do-gooder" stuff drives him nuts.

Abner Wilkes works five days a week at the central hub of Paisley • Corners: Munsie's Feed, Farm, and Farrier supply. His days are filled with the needs and wants of others—with kow-towing to Munsie and swallowing his ideas about ways to maybe do things differently. Always in the shadow of the Munsie family, especially Henry Munsie, the first-born son of Hank and Ethyl, Abner Wilkes is perpetually angry. For seventeen years, except for the days he's in charge when Munsie's away, this has been Abner's life.

But on Mondays, once the heavy snow and ice of another Caledon winter have melted, you won't find Wilkes hauling feed bags at Munsies. He'll have packed a ham'n'cheese sandwich and an apple on Sunday night and placed them on his tackle box beside his rod. And on Monday morning, Abner goes to his favourite spot on the bank of the Credit River where it flows by his place. Mud sucked at his boots, but he persisted. He needs this downtime. He's *earned* it, damn it. Rod in, morning sun, and robins flipping sweet, wet leaves. Success comes soon and often here for Abner. Today it's a Brook Trout. No swallowing. No kow-towing. A place of unfurled brows, where breath follows the calm.

On the Monday of her first scheduled visit to Abner, Kick pulled up to the old Wilkes farmstead, gravel pinging off her wheel hubs until she slowed to see if Mr. Wilkes might be outside. No one. Newspaper piles greeted her at the top of the creaky third step of a dull grey porch. No doorbell. Pulling the faded pine screen door towards her and shifting her referral folder to her other hand, Kick knocked while calling out. She waited. Behind her, a rustle preceded a faint voice: "He'll be down at the riverbank, Miss." Kick was startled, but slowly realized it was the man who she'd seen by the log home she eventually bought. She smiled warmly and eased towards the kindly man.

"Oh, it's you! How nice to see you again. I'm ..."

"Kick. I remember. I see you're all moved in, are ya?"

"Yes, yes—for quite a few months now. I was hoping I'd see you again, that you'd come around to our little farm. We've got a whole host of rescue animals now," she said and smiled.

"You won't find Abner at home," came his only reply. "It's Monday. On Mondays, he goes fishing. If you follow the path behind the house, down round the sumacs, you'll find him there, I'd wager."

Kick had dropped her folder when the friendly face first came up behind her. She bent down now to gather her things and place them in her nurse's bag, only to find her most recent acquaintance had gone. Again. She thought he'd gone off ahead of her, down the path, and so she started on her way. But instead of finding him, she came upon a fisherman standing at the riverbank. He turned at her approach. *This must be Abner*, Kick thought. The green hip waders and suspenders overtop a plaid flannel shirt with bulging buttons were possibly a clue.

"Now just who are you, young lady?" Abner demanded.

"Oh, good morning! I was looking for ... that is ... I thought I was following someone. Sorry—I'm Kick Cavendish, the public health nurse. Are you Mr. Abner Wilkes?"

"Maybe I is, maybe I ain't."

"You see, I have a referral from Dr. Dyecurt to see you for a cardiac follow-up appointment. I was at your house and, well, I learned that you might be down here by the river."

"Well, y'as found me. And as you can see, I'm just fine." Abner rummaged around in his tackle box, grumbling to himself. "Can't believe I lost my good jig in the weeds."

Recognizing that her approach needed a shift, Kick put her bags down, rolled up her pant legs, and proceeded to sit beside Mr. Wilkes on the bank, feet dangling in the water. "How's the fishing going this morning? Any brook trout biting today?"

"Mmm hmmm," muttered Abner.

"You might want to use a rooster tail or a panther martin," Kick said, pointing to the fly dangling from the fishing hook in Wilkes' hand.

He squinted his eyes and turned towards the nurse, now wringing out one of her very damp pant legs that had become unfurled. "Well, you sure know your stuff. How's it that a city girl like you knows about lure?"

Kick laughed. "I'm no city girl, and my grandpa used to take me fishing all the time in the Nottawasaga River. He had the best tackle box and loved to tell me about each and every lure and their very best use …Mr. Wilkes, how have you been feeling? Have you had any more dizzy spells?"

"Some," he offered.

Kick waited for elaboration, but none was provided. She resolved to be patient. "Do you have another rod there?"

"*You* want to fish?"

"Love to, unless you're worried I'll wreck your rod or something."

"Here, you can use my third-best one. It's light, good for, uh, girls … Do you want me to put some bait on there?"

Kick grabbed the rod and slipped a worm on the end. "I saw the robins busy with the leaves, so I turned over a few myself and *voila!*"

Together, the old-timer and the newcomer sat quietly in the morning sun, saying nothing, watching the end of their rods. She adjusted herself and settled in.

"You asked me about dizziness …"

"Yes."

"Well, it's nothing, really, but every now and then I have a bit of a problem seeing. And dang it if I'm not tired now when I get home from work." Abner paused, looked off into the distance. "That day, I couldn't see out of my left eye and I was slurring my speech. My left arm was weak. I remember because I dropped a pickle jar—a new one, with garlic. Stunk up my linoleum something awful."

"I wondered if you'd permit me to tell you a bit about TIAs, er Mini Strokes, or do you feel you are well-informed in that regard?"

"Sure, why not." Abner put down his rod, reached for his cooler, and took out his sandwich. "It's not much, but would you like to share this with me?"

"Oh, yes, that'd be great. I'm famished." She wasn't, but that didn't matter. Kick had broken through. Trust is earned. If it took eating half a sandwich even though she'd just had a large scone with jam and a coffee with her preceptor not two hours ago, so be it. She proceeded to explain causes of TIAs, after first asking Abner what his understanding was. Building off what he already knew, the skilled PHN inserted just enough information to equip him with life-saving information without overwhelming him. He is not the kind of patient to be told what to do, that's for sure.

"What do you think is best for you ... to prevent this from happening again?" she invited.

"To be bloody well taken seriously." He stopped abruptly, knowing he'd let it out. "Beg your pardon."

"Oh, that's fine, not to worry. Do you mean at work?" Kick respected the silence following her question. Opting not to probe. Opting not to repeat.

Abner hesitated. "Don't you have other visits today? I mean, I wouldn't want you to be late or anything."

"Well, yes, but we still have time. If you want to keep talking, that is."

"I think I'm about talked out. Plus, we're disturbing the fish," he chortled.

Taking cues from her patients, as much as she could, Kick agreed to complete today's visit. "Would you mind terribly if I came back again? I have a form from your doctor that he wants me to fill out, and there's still some parts in it we've not discussed."

"Sure—just not at fishing time."

CHAPTER THREE
DOTTY PINKNEY'S PRIDE

In her wartime house at the top of the hill, Dotty Pinkney hung up her apron in the same spot she always has for fifty-some years. Today, she hung it up a bit more sprightly; she didn't want to be late for her shift at the Paisley • Corners Post Office. Mrs. Mary Offenbach left last Saturday afternoon with her husband, Dolf, in their faded orange Volkswagen camper, for their annual two-week holiday. Like Mary, Dotty looked forward to those two weeks every year, but for different reasons. *Very* different reasons. For during these two weeks, and sometimes on other days here and there, Dotty became the *Substitute Postmistress*—a position she deemed to hold inordinate importance in her beloved hamlet of Paisley • Corners. Dotty had already pressed her two-piece vest and culottes outfit, after watering her garden yesterday evening, just before the mosquitoes arrived. She prided herself on being able to time her watering "just right."

Dotty prides herself on most things, but most especially on being precise and knowing something about just about everyone. Dotty married one of the founding sons of Paisley • Corners, a third cousin of her adoptive family, and resides still on a street named for her husband's uncle twice removed. It isn't unusual to find Dotty with a camera in her hand or a photo album in her arms—it being her life's work to document the comings and goings of all things Paisley • Corners.

Today, though, she had but one thing in her arms: her quilted Presbyterian Church Women bag, containing her freshly laundered Canada Post smock, her turkey and tomato sandwich, the clear plastic rain hat from a mail insert she once received, and a plum. And held tightly in her left hand was *the key*. The very same key to the post office, hanging on the Niagara Falls key chain that Mary Offenbach carried for forty-some years. Before that it was owned and carried by Mrs. Ruth Haines who together with her husband Fred, had run the post office out of the local hardware store up until "recently"—fifty years ago, that is. You see, in Paisley • Corners, fifty years ago is oft times considered recent.

Dotty piled herself and her bag into her car and drove over to the post office, where she pulled up to the parking spot out front. As she lifted herself out of her dearly departed husband's Ford Taurus, smoothing out the newly created crease on her culottes, Old Man Haines (as the locals refer to him) called out from across Main Street. "Good mornin' to ya, Miss Dotty!"

"Oh, good morning Fred," said Dotty, without looking over. "Can't talk now. It's nearly quarter to!" she exclaimed, pointing to her left wrist.

"Is it that time again already?" Fred asked. "Dolf and Mary gone out west again?"

"Hmmff," muttered Dotty. "I can't say I know where they've gone, but I *do* know I have a laundry list of things to do before I can open up these front doors. So, I'll say good morning."

Dotty always made it seem as though there was a pending stampede of stamp-needing customers awaiting her assistance. Truth be told, the post office was getting awfully slow, what with online shopping, texting, and the trend towards paperless bills and banking.

Dotty opened the post office door, only to immediately close it again from the other side, being sure to keep the blind drawn and the "Sorry, we're closed" sign undisturbed. On her way to the back room, she noted to herself how "utterly disorganized" Mary Offenbach had left things, and promptly checked to see if there was water in the kettle.

A few moments later, she heard a voice call through the front door. "Mary? Are you in there, Mary?" Olive Patterson was just outside the front door. Olive was such a gentle woman. She had lived in Paisley • Corners since marrying her "Cormie" (Mack to everyone else). Olive's husband was known to near everyone as the most helpful, drop-whatever-he's-doing-to-lend-a-hand guy around. Kind, patient, and drop-dead handsome, Cormack Patterson had longed to play pro baseball out west. But as a young buck, he caught the 4-H bug and fell in love with farming and agriculture – to which he dedicated his entire adult life. Now, his priority was his beloved wife Olive, who teetered on the edges of Alzheimer's, ever vigilant to not let on to anyone that she was slowly losing her bright, bright mind. Of course, despite her efforts, her condition was no secret to the locals.

"Mary, are you in there?" Olive called again. "I need to mail a letter to Tammy today!"

Dot put the kettle down, tucked her sandwich in the fridge, and slowly moved to open the front door. "I'm nearly ready, Olive," Dotty grudgingly answered, muttering under her breath, "Not her. Not today." Patience was *not* Dot Pinkney's strong suit. But you'd never catch her admitting that.

"Oh, Dotty, it's you," Olive noticed, somewhat startled. "Would you please open the door? It's a blasted oven out here this morning and it's not even 9 o'clock!"

"Just give me a moment," complained Dotty. Please. You see, Dotty Pinkney liked to get to her substitute postmistress position early enough to be able to look at the mail that was yet to be picked up by the delivery truck, and ... well ... gently nudge the envelopes open to take "just a quick peek." She had just set the kettle to boil when she heard the commotion at the front door. How was she ever going to be able to get to that mail pile *now* so she could find out just what was going on in Paisley • Corners? But there was no putting off Olive. Dot sighed.

"What can I do for you today, Olive?"

"I need to send my daughter a package, and it needs to get there by Friday!"

"That shouldn't be a problem; where's it going to?"

"Now, Dot, you know she lives up near Peterborough."

"Right, okay, well, we can send it via regular mail for five dollars and nineteen cents, or we can send it by express post with insurance for ten seventy-nine."

Olive rummaged around in the bottom of her purse in search of her wallet, eventually emptying the entire contents of her bag on the post office counter. Dotty was *not* impressed, and her facial expression clearly showed it. Getting Olive back from one of her increasingly frequent digressions was proving more and more difficult. "Here we go again ... " muttered Dotty under her breath. Dotty didn't have patience even on a good day, and today, when she clearly had her own plans for that stack of mail before anyone came in, she had next to none.

"There's my Bay card!" exclaimed Olive. "I've been looking for that for years! Ha. Well, whad'ya know."

"Olive ... todayyyyyyyyyy!" pushed Dotty.

"Okay, right. Sorry about that. Here you go. I'll go for the express deal."

Dotty carefully stamped the package, being sure to do so in the exact spot the Canada Post training manual indicated. She gave Olive her change and wished her a fine day, gesturing for her to leave.

Once Olive left, Dotty turned the kettle back on and started sorting through the Paisley • Corners mail to see what letters she just *had* to open. Out of the corner of her eye, a stranger passed by the post office window.

"What the …" Dotty catapulted herself towards the window to see just *who* it was. She'd never seen this young man before, but did recognize the car he got into. Bart Bignell's. "Oooh, that lizard. What on Earth is he up to now?" pondered Dotty. Bart Bignell was Paisley • Corners' best-known real estate agent. Dotty was sure that he had snakeskin seats in that "repugnant" blue Cadillac of his.

"There he goes again, squeezing money out of unsuspecting dupes," muttered Dotty. The two men, Bart and the younger man, were looking at an iPad, swiping what seemed to be images. Of what, Dotty couldn't quite make out. In unison, the men nodded, appearing to agree about something. They got back into Bart's sedan, pulled out onto the main street, and drove north.

"I wonder what *that's* about," Dot mused. "Hmm, maybe there's something about it in today's mail," she thought as she sifted and sorted some more. She faced a dilemma: Should she steam open those envelopes, or should she head on down to the local hair salon to see who knew what Bart was up to?

Dotty chose the envelopes. She couldn't help herself. She had to know what was going on. She knew it was wrong, at least on some level, but still—every time it was her turn to sub for the regular postmistress, Dotty steamed open at least a couple. She always brought glue, the kind that dried clear and without clumps. And today, she decided she'd open up one from England, even though the sight of British postage stamps made her stomach flip. It was addressed to a name she'd never heard before—a Miss Muriel Langdon with "previously of Hertfordshire" in parentheses.

Just before she steamed it, holding back the looming queasiness, another customer came in. Dotty swiftly stuffed the envelope into her smock pocket and went on with her day.

Immediately south of the post office at Bobby's Pin, the local hair salon, another drama was unfolding. Ginger Hogan, whose husband's love of darts was almost as legendary as his love for his *state-of-the-art* Septic truck, was telling all the ladies in the salon that she might hang up her scissors and comb.

"Maybe I should retire and let these new gals come in more full time," Ginger reflected.

Mabel Tarbox was in her chair, having her weekly wash and set. Same day. Same time. Same chair. Same set. "Oh Ginger, every year, you say the same thing, and every year, we all give you the same reply. Don't! So many of us have been coming to see you for years. We're used to you, and you're used to us. So what if there are new styles or new stylists. I mean, if you need to slow it down a bit for your own health or so you can spend more time with Bob, that's one thing …"

"Oh Lord, spend more time with Bob?" Ginger laughed. "I'd go deaf, he's so loud. That'd be a whole lot of husband! No, it's more that I know I'm outdated and I just don't have the energy any more to go on those week-long courses. I worry the new girls think I'm stuck in the past, or worse, that I *should* retire."

As the ladies discussed Ginger's past, present, and future, Kick pulled up outside, parked, and reviewed her next referral. She planned in her mind what she'd cover. Today, she was to do two new baby visits, which she loved. She prepared the general information package and sanitized her hands, looking out from the windshield. The hair salon was located at ground level of a street-facing historic building, and around the back of it were two separate apartments respectively marked by an A and B. Kick got out of her car, looking around to get her bearings and find the address. She felt someone looking at her and she spontaneously glanced across the street. Her eye was drawn to an upper window where she just managed to catch a glimpse of a woman's face. As suddenly as the feeling came that someone was looking at her, a yellowed lace drape was moved to cover the window; the woman's shadow retreated from sight.

Kick made her way to the back of the salon building and Unit A's fire escape stairs. As she navigated their twisting steepness, she worried about the safety of a new mom going up and down them with a babe in arms. A stroller was outside just next to the stairs but was wet and a bit dirty. Processing her new patient's surroundings, Kick considered additional issues that might be faced by a new mom here in a rural hamlet. She knocked on the door. No response. She tapped on the window and called in, announcing who she was. When again she received no reply, she made her way back down the black, wrought-iron staircase, reminded of similar spiral stairways she'd seen in Montreal.

Kick popped her head into the hair salon about to ask if anyone knew where her patient was, and Ginger greeted her. "Hello there, Kick. Are you in need of a blow-dry? I've got time. You've got such thick and lovely hair."

"Oh Ginger, thank you. I wish I had time. I wondered if anyone knew where the woman who lives upstairs might be? She just had a baby, I believe?"

Ginger Hogan made it her business to know who lived upstairs— not to be nosy, but to be of help. "You mean Denise? A cab picked her up over an hour ago. I think she goes to see the doctor by cab. I don't believe she has a car. Not one that I've ever seen. I saw her hand the little one to the cab driver as she got into the back seat."

Just then a car door closed out front and a woman walked by, holding an infant.

"Ah, I think that just might be my patient," said Kick with a delighted smile. "I'll be off then." She hurried to the back of the building, hoping to help the young mom, but she was already halfway up the stairs. Once Kick's new patient was in, the nurse made her way up the stairs and gently tapped on the door again.

"Come on in," a tired voice called out.

"Thank you," Kick replied, opening the door and peeping in. "You must be Denise. Sorry to come in just as you were arriving. I'll let you get settled."

Rail thin, with a faded dress that had seen better days, Denise checked her hair in the hallway mirror, and quickly closed a bedroom door. "You must be the health nurse. I'm sorry I am a bit late for our appointment; the baby had her first weigh in today."

"How's she doing? Did we have a gain?"

"Yes; not enough, but still, a gain. Let me put her down and I'll put the kettle on."

Kick took it upon herself to fill the kettle and washed out two cups from the sink. In the strainer was a manual breast pump and two bottles.

Denise came into the kitchen. "Okay, she's tired. We'll have time to talk, which is good."

Once the tea was served, Kick asked her patient how things were going for her, and whether she had any concerns or things she wanted to specifically discuss.

"Not really," came the reply.

With that, Kick took out the Healthy Babies Health Children referral form and explained her role and the non-compulsory nature of PHN home visits. "How about I go through some of the usual questions and we will see if that spurs on any questions on your part?"

With a mutually agreed upon plan in place for today's visit, Kick journeyed through some of the various topics PHNs cover and assess during new baby visits, making note of any possible community resources to mention at a suitable time.

DOB, Birth History, Family Consistency
Weight
Urine output
Stool output, consistency, stages
Infant Feeding Assessment
Breastfeeding Assessment:
Initiation, Position, Latch, Signs of effective feeding
Hand Expression Method
Formula: Type Amount, Frequency
Sterilization, Preparation, Storage
Safe Sleep Teaching
Prenatal history, classes
Availability of Family Support/Parenting partner
Links to Social Supports
Response to the baby, previous losses, other children
Maternal health concerns

"Why do you think she's not gaining enough?" Denise suddenly interjected. Kick explained the variety of possible reasons, including latch and maternal nutrition. Denise looked guilty. "Yes, I don't eat much. Rent is very expensive, and I'm on my own."

With that disclosure, Kick resolved to focus on making sure her patient wasn't blaming herself inadvertently for the baby not gaining as much weight as the doctor would want. "Are you linked to any resources? Financial? Food-wise?"

"No."

"Shall I tell you about what I know is available for new moms?"

"Sure, I guess so."

Kick reviewed her list and then initiated referrals to local community resources that would ensure her patient had access to financial supports.

Rubbing her forehead in thought, Denise replied, "There's just so much to learn."

Sensing her patient's change in body language, Kick shifted the focus of the visit to Denise's sense of worth and highlighted a litany of strengths and skills that the new mom was showing to her public health nurse. Slowly, a smile filled out the young woman's rosy face. Kick reached out her hand, placing it on Denise's. "You've got this. One day at a time. One pamphlet at a time. You're no different than all the other mothers out there. Trust in yourself. And if you're okay with me coming a few times a week, we can make sure both you and Amy are feeling well and thriving."

Kick left her card, an information package that included the New Parents' Helpline, and scheduled another home visit in three days' time. On her way home from her second new baby visit, Kick stopped by Unit A again and dropped off a new mom care package from community services, hugging her patient reassuringly as she let herself out.

Public health nurses strive to understand the lives, dreams, wishes, and sorrows of a community—or what is more formally referred to as the nurse's aggregate. So much is discussed over tea during the formal, structured visit, whatever its official reason. But even more so, especially if the PHN manages to make the coveted connection with a client, it's when you place your hand on the doorknob about to leave, that so much more is often shared. PHNs learn to pivot, pause and listen.

With Madeline Prescott, Kick learned all she needed to within twenty minutes of standing together in her tiny kitchen. Madeline, or Maddie as most Paisley • Corners folks call her, is the sunniest person you'll ever want to meet. Kick's visits to Maddie focused on making sure she was linked to all the community services she might desire so she could stay secure in her own home. But in the back of Kick's mind, she had another motive: she longed to know Maddie's secret to happiness. How does Maddie manage to stay in the light, despite hard times or worrisome events? Kick believes that PHNs learn something from every person they visit, and she felt affected by the unspoken wisdom of this independent lady, who'd won numerous town awards for her volunteering and giving back. Kick liked her. Very much. And while it's not a goal or a requisite that PHNs like all their clients, Maddie's sunny disposition always made Kick feel lighter.

"You seem a bit down, dear," Maddie offered on that first afternoon, when Kick's hand met the doorknob on her way out.

"Oh, I'm sorry Maddie. Really? Uh, sorry. No."

"What's wrong? Maybe I can help?"

"You're a funny one. I mean, who is the nurse, anyway?" Kick asked.

"Well … am I right?"

"Yes, well, Caleb and I did recently lose one of our rescues. I try to put it to the side and just press on, but my mind drifted, while you were clearing the tea, to our little goat Olivia. I am really going to miss her."

"Oh, I understand," Maddie said, gazing at Kick with sympathy. "It's so nice—what you're doing, I mean. I don't know how you get it all done. I'm sorry you lost her. I'm sure she felt loved. Just let your feelings come in. Don't fight them. Remember: grief is the cost we pay for love."

Kick was jarred by the profundity of this tiny woman's life lesson, offered at the doorstep. Usually, it was the PHN imparting the wisdom, or so she'd learned in nursing school. Kick again felt thankful for her patient, for Paisley • Corners and, yes, for the loving relationships with all her rescues — a love that is always concluded by grief.

CHAPTER FOUR
MALCOLM AND AMBROSE

Malcolm Putney has walked his brother Ambrose everywhere. He walked him to his first day at school. He walked him to Sunday school at the Paisley • Corners Presbyterian church, down steep and often slippery wooden stairs to the basement. He even walked his brother three-quarters of the way to Loretta McAvoy's house that first Saturday afternoon to call on her. Ambrose waved him off, but Malcolm got close enough to see if her father was on the porch. When he saw that only apple-cheeked, fifteen-year-old Loretta and a pitcher of fresh lemonade were there on the porch, he made his way back home. Over their sixty-plus years together, Malcolm and Ambrose Putney walked pretty much everywhere together.

Just a few years back, Malcolm walked his brother back to their blue Ford F-350 through the muddy path made by all the town mourners. Some say Ambrose Putney's never been the same since his beloved Loretta died so suddenly after making him her famous raisin pie. The oven was still warm from the pie when Ambrose accidentally leaned on it as he searched for the phone to call the ambulance. Ambrose hated that phone. "Whatever possessed them damn engineer types to dream up a phone not connected to the wall?" he'd say to Loretta. "I can't never find the blasted thing. At least when it was attached to the wall, I'd always know where it was."

Nowadays, Ambrose doesn't use the phone. He doesn't need it. Ambrose doesn't do much, truth be told. He's got Malcolm, just like when they were kids, and that suits them both just fine. He doesn't even go to Munsie's Feed, Farm and Farrier Supply, the place where nearly all the men of Paisley • Corners congregate, especially during the slower months when all the seeds have been sown or when the farmlands go dormant during the winter. Today, a cold Thursday in March, the Putney brothers needed feed for their horse and chickens, so someone needed to go to Munsie's. Ambrose made a list and left it beside his brother's favorite Montreal Canadians coffee mug, stained and well-used. The brothers used to do these sorts of things together, but not anymore. Ambrose barely left the farmhouse now. And so Malcolm set out in the cold morning sun.

"How's tricks with you, Malcolm?" welcomed Munsie, the owner of the feed store. "How's that brother of yours? We never see him no more."

Malcolm was still kicking off the snow from the size eleven boots he got on sale last spring. Malcom's feet were size nine. "Fair to middlin," he replied. "Fair to middlin."

He warmed his hands at the wood stove, being careful not to rub off the cracked skin between his fingers that he tried to conceal when ladies were around. Like at church and all.

"Hey, did ya forget your gloves, Malcolm?" chided Abner Wilkes, Munsie's second in command. "It's one bitter wind out there this morning, I tell ya."

"Somethin' like that," muttered Malcolm quietly. Malcolm could usually pace his walk to the feed-n-farm supply near perfect so his hands wouldn't freeze. But not this morning. This morning, as he walked across the field behind his farm and down across Poplar

Sideroad, he was delayed. No. He was stunned. Seven black crows. The last time he saw that many crows hovering overhead, Millie had died. Millie was the blue-eyed grey mare Ambrose had bought for Loretta as a wedding present. She was found near froze in the field, giving birth to her first and only foal, Blaze, and for hours, the crows circled until the brothers Putney were able to get her picked up. For weeks, Ambrose stopped working. Stopped eating, stopped talking, stopped living. If only he had gotten there before his beloved Loretta to spare her that sight. But Loretta, being Loretta, took care of Blaze, bottle feeding him, sleeping beside him, being a substitute mother to him. She took care of that entire farm, and pushed Ambrose to believe in himself more, instead of accepting his family's loving goal of a shielded existence.

Then, today, the triggering sight of seven black crows again. Malcolm panicked. "Oh no, oh no—not Blaze!" He ran as fast as seventy-year-old legs in size eleven boots could take him, back to the Putney farm to check on things. Once he saw Blaze out in the pasture beside their rescue donkey, Eddie, both of them looking up at the commotion, Malcolm stopped running. He caught his breath and headed back to the feed store.

It may have been the first day of spring but the trails and trees of Paisley • Corners remained snow covered. Despite a wicked wind-chill, the cardinals were calling. Back and forth. Back and forth. As spring approached these past two weeks, so too did the hues of blue in the Caledon sky. While last week Malcolm could see right across Caledon's portion of the Niagara Escarpment, today low cloud cover appeared within reach, touching treetops and hill tops. It was a morning of hope and promise – of pending growth and of survival after the bleak and beauty that characterizes winter on Ontario's snow belt.

"Help yourself to a coffee there, Malcolm," Munsie said. "You look near frozen." And so he did. "Can I get ya anything this morning?"

Malcolm was warming his hands by the woodstove. "Well now, lemme think. I need some cracked corn, and uh, some supplement and some straw."

"Ten pounds do ya? And a five-bale?"

"Uh, no, just gimme two pounds and one bale," Malcolm said, his voice slowly draining. He coughed, warmed his hands some more, and reached for his wallet.

"Okay there Malcolm, debit or credit?"

Continually frustrated with that question but not wanting to let on, Malcolm glanced out the window to take stock of the weather situation for his walk home. He placed a twenty-spot on the wooden counter, smiling. Malcolm *always* paid cash.

"How's bout we deliver this to you fellas later this morning?"

"Well now, that'll be just fine." Malcolm adjusted his hat, pulled the sleeves of his long underwear as long as he could get them, and prepared to set out again back to the Putney homestead.

"Hey," said Munsie, "why don't you take a traveler? Sure is a cold walk yer facin."

"Well now, don't mind if I do."

Abner Wilkes cleared his throat with a sly, tight-lipped smile. Ignoring him, Malcolm filled the John Deere paper cup again with coffee, re-adjusted his sleeves, and fastened the lid tight so's he'd not spill any before he gave it to Ambrose back home.

Everyone knew about the Putney Farm falling on hard times, but no one ever said a thing. Not to the Putney brothers, at least. The Putney family had done so much for so long for so many folks in Paisley • Corners; many would say they've earned the charade that the entire town accepts.

Malcolm made his way home, pulling his coat collar tighter to block the wind. Stomping off the snow from his boots and leaving them on the boot tray, Malcolm called up to his brother, "There's a coffee there for ya,"

"Okay, be right dowwnnn!" Ambrose answered.

Ambrose was a bit slower these days, ever since his dear, sweet Loretta died. Underestimated, acquiescent, with not a mean bone in his increasingly flaccid body, he appreciated all his brother ever did for him, even if deep down Ambrose knew he could do more than he was permitted.

Ambrose had been born with mild cerebral palsy, and his family had worked to shield him from hardship; Malcolm was charged with holding a metaphorical umbrella over his brother's life. Growing up, "Look out for your brother" was the single most common phrase directed at Malcolm: at breakfast, out in the fields on the Putney farm, at Sunday school, wherever. And Malcolm did this with nary an ounce of resentment. It just was. Wherever Ambrose was, Malcolm was close behind or right there beside him. They had bunk beds as children, and since Ambrose couldn't walk too well or climb, one leg and arm being weakened by his birth injury, the lower bunk was, of course, his. To this day, has Malcolm never let his brother know he was deathly afraid of heights as a child. He just makes sure Ambrose is safe. Always.

Many of the kids assumed Ambrose was "simple." "Slow." "Stupid." Any number of offensive terms were thrown around about him, especially by Abner Wilkes, his worst enemy since the first day Ambrose went to Paisley • Corners public school. Truth be told, Ambrose can remember almost every time that Abner pushed him down, called him a "retard," or made sure he was chosen *last* for dodge ball or shinny or red rover. To top it all off, Abner had always longed to have Loretta McAvoy on *his* arm, and when she chose Ambrose to be her betrothed, the last ounce of niceness Abner might've had towards him evaporated.

Second in line to Loretta, *second* in command at the feed store, too. He's never hidden his displeasure with his lot in life – not now and not back in school either. And while the man's overt bully days are all but over, Ambrose is sure he felt the sneer of Abner on the back of his plaid work jacket whenever he "hobbled" to the far corner of the feed supply store to get some cracked corn for "his girls."

"Munsie asked fer ya," Malcolm said, after Ambrose had made his way down the stairs.

Where'd ya say the coffee was?" replied Ambrose.

"There, beside your Leafs mug. You'll need to warm it up. It was a cold walk today."

Ambrose is a *huge* Leafs fan—Toronto Maple Leafs, that is—and has had the same white, transparent Leafs mug for some thirty years. He loves this mug. It's a little like him, sorta. Seemingly weak and fragile, but proving itself time and time again as able to withstand all sorts of traumas.

Ambrose poured the coffee out of the beat-up John Deere paper coffee cup and into his favourite mug, and warmed it up in the microwave.

"What was all the commotion before?" Ambrose asked his brother. "I saw ya runnin.'"

"Oh," replied Malcolm, "I thought I heard Blaze stuck again in the fence. But it was nuthin.' You hungry? How about a bacon and tomato sandwich?" When Ambrose nodded, Malcolm set to making lunch for them—two bacon and tomato sandwiches, only one of which had any bacon on it—humming a tune that had been playing on the radio at Munsie's.

Malcolm loves the oldies, and the radio has played continuously in the Putney kitchen for decades and decades. And as the two brothers sat in their farmhouse kitchen and had lunch, as they have done so many times before, they found themselves reminiscing ...

"Remember how Ma and Pa used to sit right here and eat bacon sandwiches, and Ma would give Pa her bacon near every time?" recalled Ambrose.

"Mmm hmm," Malcolm agreed, while writing the grocery list. "What do we need, Ambrose? I'm going to Foodville later on."

"Bananas, milk, Sanka and, um, something else," Ambrose recalled, pushing his chair away from the table and getting up to go to the bathroom.

"That's ok, I think there's another list I started last night watchin' the game. It's probably right here on the table somewhere ..."

Seems everything was on that table. Bills, last week's *Caledon Times* newspaper, half-done crosswords, the Leafs' schedule, lists of things to do on the farm, and a notice from the propane company about a rate increase.

It was this notice that had Malcolm tossing and turning at night. How was he to keep their old, drafty farmhouse warm enough for his brother's condition? Years of falling had left Ambrose terribly arthritic and Malcolm, being Malcolm, wanted to at least try to keep those joints as limber as possible. Having the house warm, he hoped, was at least one way.

His worries were interrupted. "Soup!!" Ambrose called out from the upstairs washroom. "I knew there were something else," he muttered.

"Well now, that'll be just fine!" replied Malcolm, still thumbing the propane notice. He knew he needed propane, but also knew his brother needed his prescription re-filled *and* they needed food for the animals and themselves.

Just then, Malcolm heard Blaze whinny from across the yard. He looked out the kitchen window through the tattered kitchen curtain to see Munsie's truck just pulling up. He threw his coat and boots on again and went out to meet young Jamie Munsie, the second eldest son, who everyone in PC knew was set to inherit the supply outfit when his dad was ready to retire.

48

"Good day to ya, there Malcolm," Jamie called out.

"Mornin' lad," Malcolm replied.

"And how's everyone at the farm? How's Ambrose and his girls? I see Blaze is up and frisky as ever. He was trying to get Eddie to run around with him." Jamie smiled.

"Fair to middlin; just hungry is all," smiled Malcolm gently. Together, Jamie Munsie and Malcolm brought in the straw and the cracked corn. Just when Malcolm thought they were done, Jamie took down a bag of horse feed and some hay.

"Hold on there lad—I'm sorry to make you have to lift all that agin,' but I dares say we didn't order any hay or any other feed," cautioned Malcolm.

"Oh," Jamie struggled to explain, "my Dad put this on the truck and wondered if you could use it for Blaze. He said our mare and her foals won't touch it and since it's already opened, we can't sell it. We needed to make room in the loft for next summer's first cut, and we're trying to get rid of the leftover hay and straw. Dad thought you could use the straw for the girls' egg boxes and the hay for Blaze," he struggled to explain with a straight face.

"Alright," Malcolm answered, avoiding eye contact. He was afraid that they'd figured it out. But then again, the Munsies are such a generous family, always lending a hand to just about every farm in Paisley • Corners that this wasn't *unlike* Munsie.

"Where should I put it, Malcolm?"

"Oh, right, let's put it here in the feed room." And with that, young Jamie Munsie stacked ten bales of hay, four bales of straw and not one, but two bags of horse feed in the feed room. The young man tried to not show any reaction to the emptiness of the feed room, but in his heart, he felt glad that his dad had done this for the brothers. "Ok there, Malcolm, I'll be on my way. They say there's another storm coming, and I've got a few more deliveries."

And with that, Jamie was off in what was probably PC's most recognizable truck—next to Bob the septic guy's, that is.

When Malcolm came back into the house, Ambrose was limping out onto the back porch, where they kept their apple cider and other things they wanted kept cold but not frozen. "Need help?" Ambrose asked his brother.

"Nope. All done," answered Malcolm reassuringly. He always tries to get the heavy lifting done before his brother even has the chance to offer his help. It isn't because Ambrose *can't* do it. It's just that Malcolm always tries to spare him of any chances that he might fall. "Let's have that coffee now. I'll warm it up again for ya."

The two brothers took to their respective chairs and once again, Ambrose took to reminiscing. "I remember when old man Munsie used'a bring Ma and Pa their feed. Young Jamie reminds me of his grandpa, that's fer sure. Friendly as all get-out. Always havin' time to give ya, even with a full truck and a list of deliveries as long as his arm."

Back when Jamie's grandpa ran Munsie's, some forty years ago, the Putney farm was a prosperous one. Hay in the fields, eggs to sell, pullets for sale every spring, and jars and jars of preserves prepared for a long cold winter. The two boys had good boots in the winter and new sneakers in the summer.

Mrs. Putney was involved in the Women's Institute, and she sure appreciated the time she took for it, as she learned about any number of things going on in the world. Back then, the Women's Institute was known for educating farm wives, and many a branch of the institute took to lobbying governments for things like school milk programs, subsidies on farm equipment for food producers, and better supports for children living on Indigenous reserves.

Mr. Putney was an elder in the Presbyterian church and for decades, was the head usher overseeing the collection plates, turning on and off the lights, locking the doors after the service, and, once every June, with helping out at the annual Steak Barbecue. Mr. Putney liked to think he was a shrewd gentleman, but the truth is he was gentle, trusting, and always liked to see the best in others and in situations others might see as full of doom and gloom.

It was Mr. Putney who only half believed the forecast limitations that the doctors spoke of when Ambrose was born on a dull day in early April. It was a long and tough labor; Malcolm, being just shy of ten years old, climbed to the second loft of the barn trying to avoid hearing his mother wail. "He's so blue," Mrs. Putney cried when she first saw Ambrose. "Why is he so blue? He's not crying. Dear Lord, do something!" she implored of the doctor. With no portable oxygen, the doctor and attending nurse frantically rubbed the baby's back to get him to gulp air while moving him nearer to the bedroom window.

Ambrose suffered what doctors called birth anoxia, caused from a kink in the umbilical cord that was barely seen in a dimly lit back bedroom on the Putney farm. With his head protruding and the darkened blue tinge evident, the doctor precipitously reached in and gently removed the slightly folded twist. From that very moment, the entire Putney family set their sights on watching over Ambrose and working to prevent any and all troubles. "When I'm not here, you're the man of the house," Malcolm's father would tell him. "Stay close to your brother," Ambrose's mom would say, adding, "Now, Malcolm, you take him with you. Keep a close eye. He's ... well, watch out for him, okay?"

It would seem that the birth anoxia caused Ambrose's brain to selectively communicate with *some* of his muscles, but not others. And so, Ambrose walked with a limp, and one arm was a bit weak and not very flexible. He'd fall. A lot. It didn't bother him much. But it worried Mrs. Putney to dyspepsia, it did. At times, Ambrose would speak slower than the other children, with periodic slurs or seeming gaps in comprehension. He learned, but just a bit slower and a bit differently than most of the kids.

Later on in life, Mrs. Putney would tell her husband how her heart would pain her when she let herself worry about how Ambrose would get on once she died. "What if he's at the train crossing? What if he's in the barn and Francis doesn't see him and then rears up? What if ..." and then Mr. Putney would interrupt in frustration. But then he'd collect himself before criticizing her or being unkind, for he'd see her eyes—her guilt-ridden eyes. And with that, he'd lay his hand on hers, saying nothing while saying everything.

You see, Mrs. Putney blamed herself for Ambrose's troubles. Malcolm hated how his mother would worry. He loved her so ... And Malcolm being Malcolm, well, he took it upon himself to do whatever she wanted him to do for his brother. He'd take Ambrose with his friends when they'd go to Boyce's creek, or to Dick's dam, or to the pinnacle near Shaw's creek. He'd take his little brother to the fairgrounds when it was time for the 4H show. He even took him on his first date. Malcolm's, that is. The girl wasn't too impressed, so, it was, well ... his last date—at least, with her. If anyone Malcolm was friends with didn't accept Ambrose, well, they simply wouldn't be friends anymore. Not that Malcolm would be mean or anything. It's just that they were a package deal, so to speak. And on the morning when his mother was about to face her maker, Malcolm promised her she'd never have to worry about Ambrose, for he'd always look out for his brother. Especially now that his father had been dead for two years. Hearing that reassurance, she smiled weakly, closed her eyes, and gently took her last breath.

"I'm on my way now. Be back soon," called Malcolm from the front step. Ambrose was dozing on and off in the kitchen in one of their matching La-Z-boy recliners. He was especially tired today after being up most of the night with aching legs. As he dozed, he kept warm beside the stove. The brothers often set their stove to two hundred and fifty degrees, opened the door, and let the oven heat warm the kitchen, where they now most often sat. Their television was on the kitchen counter, and their radio was on the windowsill, just a hair below the lowest edge of the faded calico kitchen drapes their mother had sewn so long ago.

Malcolm set off to run some errands for the farm. His brother needed his prescription refilled; they also needed some groceries and—unfortunately—some gas in their truck. Later that week, his brother also had his physiotherapy appointment—a necessary expense, given that his tendons keep shortening, reducing his mobility all the more. This and so many other things worried Malcolm. He was, after all, ten years older, and despite working so hard to stay healthy so he could be there always for his brother, he knew he'd probably go first.

Malcolm slowly drove down their long driveway, trying his best to watch for any chickens that might be on it. He took the short stretch of the Number Two Sideroad and then turned north onto the main street. He waved to Ginger Hogan, who was having a smoke outside her hair salon, and she called out, "Hey there, Malcolm. When are we going to see you and that brother of yours? You're lookin' as though you could use a cleanup!" Malcolm smiled and proceeded on, turning left into the gas station.

"'Ow she cutting d'ere b'y?" Gus greeted him.

"Fair to middlinn'.' Except for the price of gas these days."

"Yes b'y. Buddy's snapped right off, he is. Whoever makes up dese prices."

"Twenty dollars, if ya don't mind."

Gus filled Malcom's gas tank, being sure to stand in front of the pump while he filled it to thirty dollars' worth. "There's ya go dere, Malcolm. Says hello to Ambrose. I'll drop over 'round by and by."

"Sure, sure." With that, Malcolm drove off up the hill towards the grocery store. He parked away from the main area, where the drug store, dry cleaners, physio office and bakeshop was, mostly because his truck was so large. He also didn't want to take up a spot for someone who couldn't walk as well as he could. Spry, he is, even though he's seventy. Before leaving his truck, Malcolm grabbed the four coupons he had clipped held together with a paper clip, hopped down, and closed the door, not bothering to lock it.

He grabbed a mini-buggy and when he entered the store, he was greeted by young Tanis Eccles, the twenty-something nursing student who has been working at Foodville since she was fourteen. "Morning Mr. Putney," Tanis called out. "We've got Ambrose's favourite bread just fresh out of the oven. I'll grab you one before they're all gone. And we just filled up the specials bin, too." Malcolm liked to go to the specials bin right away, often choosing meat or veggies or anything that was discounted by fifty percent. Malcolm was taught early in life how to look for bargains, but ever since the Putney farm fell on hard times, he's been all the more frugal.

Twenty-odd years ago, developers discovered Paisley • Corners. And unlike Kick Cavendish, who discovered its beauty, serenity, and its gentle way of communal living, the developers discovered its numerous lucrative natural resources. Woodlots, aggregate and acres and acres of developable farmland, Paisley • Corners was a treasure trove for extraction companies. One day, Malcolm was in the barn mucking out the stalls when an unusual car pulled up the driveway. He brushed himself off, adjusted his cap, and exited the barn to greet the strangers stepping out of the car.

"Good morning, Sir," one of them said. "I'm Michael Baron and this is my intern, Josh Brandt. We're with Hill View Inc. Might we have a moment of your time?" Malcolm, being Malcolm, invited the two men to the front porch, where he brought them some lemonade and some of the cookies Jo Fraser had dropped off earlier that week.

The conversation started off pretty simple, with their observations of how pretty Paisley • Corners and the surrounding area were and how their company was wanting to, as Michael Baron put it, "give back to farmers who had given so much to Ontario." He told Malcolm, "We want to help farmers who are older, like yourself, to be financially set in their retirement. We are willing to buy your property and pay you a fine and fair sum, all the while letting you live right here in your own home, with five surrounding acres for your animals. And then when the time comes, and let's hope the good Lord doesn't call you up too soon, we would do whatever it is you want with your house."

Malcolm stared out to his fields—fields once filled with corn and hay and soybeans—letting their offer sink in. Just then, he heard an awful bang, followed by a meager groan … It was Ambrose. He had fallen again. The businessmen opened up their leather attaché cases and pulled out a contract with Malcolm's name already on it, as well as the lot, plan, and concession number of the Putney farm. "Malcolm—can I call you Malcolm? —we know you have a disabled brother to think about. We want to help you with that too, as you're both not getting any younger. We've drawn up a contract for you to look at. How's bout we leave it with you, and come back to see you tomorrow?"

"Well, now, I don't know. Tomorrow's a might soon. We country folk don't do things so speedy-like. Plus, I'll have to talk to my brother about this and give it some thought. Say, just how do you know about my brother?"

"Malcolm, everyone knows about the Putney Brothers and how central your whole family has been in Parsnip Corners."

"Uh, that's Paisley • Corners."

"Right, right, sorry, it's been a long drive and an even longer day."

Unbeknownst to Malcolm, the team from Hillview had been all over Caledon to bring prepared contracts to four other farmers.

Malcolm shook their hands and explained the best way to get back to the highway and head south to the city. After the strangers drove off, he gathered the papers and put them under the pile of bills on the kitchen table, checked on Ambrose, who was now asleep in his recliner, and set himself down in front of the oven to think ...

The contract got signed. The deal was done. And the bulldozers had come. Of the hundred acres sold to Hillview, sixty or so were beautiful woodlots. Within two weeks, the woodlots were gone, and flatbed after flatbed came and went with hundreds of logs strapped in. Phone calls went unanswered. Letters went ignored. Surveyors marked the Putney's remaining acreage of fields, streams and ponds for where the best aggregate could be found.

Then, one day, there was a knock at the door: "Delivery for Mr. Malcolm Putney," said the gentleman in the brown jacket and pant uniform. "Sign here, please, Mr. Putney." And in the cardboard envelope was a one-page letter informing Malcolm that Hillview Inc. was no more. Bankrupt. He dug to the bottom of the envelope, hoping to find a cheque. Nothing. The Putney farm would never farm again. The fields were ruined. The watershed all but drained dry. The woodlot desecrated. And Malcolm, being Malcolm, blamed himself, and has run himself ragged trying to keep the truth of their finances from Ambrose.

After Malcolm loaded his car with groceries, he noticed a sign out front of the Paisley • Corners Bake Shop: *75ᵗʰ Anniversary Celebration --- Join Us for Free Coffee.*

"I don't think the milk'll spoil," Malcolm muttered to himself. So over he went to set a spell and have a coffee and a plain donut. He'd bring Ambrose a coffee and one of the apple fritters their bakery was known for.

"Here for the free grub, are ya Putney?" sneered Abner Wilkes as soon as Malcolm walked in the door.

"Well now, I suppose I am." Malcolm sat down to read one of the left-over Toronto papers a passer-through probably left.

"Hmmph," Wilkes muttered. He returned to his pretty near one-sided conversation with Cormack Patterson. "I hear he's won himself some awards for some new way to predict harvest time. But that 'aint the whole of it. I hear tell he's got himself one of them mail order brides. The kind who's understandin'… if ya know what I mean."

"Uh huh. Always good to talk to you Abner," Mack stated, horrified with Abner's ignorance. Having tried twice already to get away from Abner, he pushed open the bakery door, saying, "I better be getting back. Olive will be wondering where I've gotten to. She worries something fierce these days. Afternoon, Malcolm."

"Afternoon, Mack. Have a good one. Regards to Miss Olive." Malcolm relaxed into the chair and started to read the paper, uncharacteristically staying for a refill of coffee and a second section of the *Toronto Star*. Checking his watch, he began to worry less about the milk in the truck and more about how Ambrose was. Malcolm brought his dishes to the front of the bakery, tipped his cap to the friendly cashier, and rummaged for his keys in his pocket.

Just then, the pager on the belt of one of the gents buying a cup of coffee went off; he was out the door in seconds and into his truck, onto which he placed a blue flashing light as he drove off.

"Must be a fire," Malcolm heard the busboy say. Malcolm suddenly got a bad feeling. He set off down the hill, back to the main core of the hamlet and past the three and a half corners. His mind wandered for just a moment, worried that something might've happened to Ambrose because he took so long at the bakery. Turning down the side road and toward his driveway, Malcom's heart sank with the sight of the Paisley • Corners fire truck and pumper wagon down by the house.

Forty-five minutes prior, Old Joe had been carrying some wood he'd cut from a fallen tree on the Caledon Trailway. He often brought wood to the Putney brothers, leaving it on their back porch when no one was around. But today, he smelled smoke. The neighbours must've smelled it, too, and called 911. Old Joe tried to call into the house, but he barely had a voice, since he rarely spoke to anyone. "Anyone here?" he shouted in a raspy voice. He opened the back kitchen door and smoke came drifting out.

"Joe? Is that you, Joe?" replied Ambrose, weakly.

"Yes, it's me. Where are you? I can hardly see two feet in front of me."

"I'm in the living room. I fell trying to get out of the kitchen and I've twisted my ankle."

Old Joe ran around to the front of the house, pushed past the white screen door, and groped his way toward Ambrose in the smoke. He pulled Ambrose out the front, away from the smoke and fire in the kitchen.

By the time Malcolm got out of his truck, he could see his brother sitting on the bench by the small apple orchard in the front acreage. Malcolm breathed a sigh of relief, but only for a minute. The one last thing they had was on fire. He shouldn't have left. He shouldn't have stayed for a second coffee. He shouldn't have read the paper.

Theodore Buckett, the OPP Detachment Commander, approached him. "The boys have the fire out, Malcolm. There's a lot of smoke damage and it seems your oven is *kaput*, but other than that, you boys can be back in there later today."

Malcolm nodded. He decided to check on the animals in the barn and clean it out while the house cleared out. But rather than clean the barn, Malcolm just stared out, one arm on the shovel and the other arm leaning on the bottom half of the barn door. Blaze nuzzled him and stole his handkerchief. A resident chipmunk ran over his boots to get to some of the scratch he had dropped. Cornelius, their rooster, announced that it was two p.m. Nothing shook him from his pensiveness until a large and warm hand set down on his thinning shoulder: "Malcolm, don't you worry yourself a bit. We'll have that kitchen set to rights before you know it." And Cormack Patterson meant it.

CHAPTER FIVE
THE RETURN OF THE LAVENDER TRILLIUM

Jo Fraser sipped her tea, flipping through the Milk Calendar she had just taken down from her cork board. She was trying to decide when—not if—she'd have the hip surgery her doctor's been trying to arrange. "I'm just busy, she'd say."

"Just give me three measly months," he'd plead, "and you can get right back to all your shenanigans."

So Jo flipped the calendar ... May, June ... and flipped ... July, August ... and flipped some more. Until. There it was: October ninth, the day she's drawn a birthday balloon on since she was eight years old. *He'll be seventy-five this year,* she thought, rubbing her Royal Albert Country Roses teacup with an arthritically disfigured thumb.

Deep in thought, Jo glanced out her window and became breathless at the sight of the lavender grey trilliums growing in the shady spot of her yard. Hand to chest, Jo tried to take it in stride, but couldn't. Even after so many returning springs, she still couldn't. The sight of these rare flowers brought her back to her childhood and back to a deep longing for a beloved best friend she'd long lost contact with. The only other place she's ever seen lavender grey trillium was in the shaded crevices of the Cheltenham Badlands—and even then, only when she would spend hours there with Charlie. She knows for sure she's never planted trillium in her back yard, and also that she's never picked them. Born and raised in Ontario, Jo felt it wasn't ok to pick trillium. Even though in 2009 the law prohibiting it was taken off the books, like everyone else around here, the obligation to protect Ontario's flower stayed firm.

Jo put her faded yellow garden smock on and her even yellower Wellies and went out her back porch door. Oscar, her latest adopted stray cat, managed to make it out just in time before the screen door slammed shut. She just had to see them up close. Even though her eyes are cloudy and beginning to fail, she just had to greet them hand to petal. *How lovely,* she thought.

In high school, she studied the Badlands as an independent project, learning that the minerals found in the exposed Queenston shale created the rarity that is the lavender grey colour. Without the shale, a trillium would bloom brilliant white, pale pink, or luxurious burgundy. She just loved the lavender grey blooms, and despite the mystery surrounding their arrival years ago, she promised herself she'd just accept them as a gift from God.

After delicately grazing the flowers with her fingertips, Jo steadied herself on the side of her potting shed bracing for the pending pain as she raised herself up off her gardener's mat. Her left hip was especially sore of late, and today being the 24th of May (May Two-Four for

Canadians), it was going to be even worse given all the planting she needed to do.

The first time that Kick saw the Badlands was by accident on her way to visit a 'shut-in' whose family had given up on him decades ago. "You've got to let it go," they'd say. "It wasn't your fault. They were playing chicken. Move on, man. Turn the blasted page." Keith Morris had driven transport since he was twenty-one, starting out on long hauls from Ontario to Vancouver or Ontario to New Brunswick. He prided himself for his safety record, with never an accident and his rigs always passing safety checks. He didn't pride himself for much else, as, unlike his siblings, Keith never married and didn't have children. The road was his family, he'd say, hoping to get the focus off his life's supposed shortcomings, identified often during family gatherings.

One autumn day, he was returning home from a shorter trip to Quebec, looking forward to watching the hockey game with a cold one. Detoured to a bi-pass due to road construction, Keith slowed to the limit of 80 kms an hour. At first, he was convinced his eyes deceived him. Was that … was that *kids* on the road????? He tried to slow down and let out his horn, but they kept darting on and off the road. He eventually stopped, but it was too late. He got out. He tried to help. He wanted to help, but there was nothing he could do. And there beside his rig, his body collapsed and, alongside of it, so did his soul.

The public health nurse who used to work in Quebec and was assigned to the area where this tragedy occurred told Kick about that day, lamenting on how little the focus was on the driver. "He never returned to work, moved to Ontario and has been holed up in his Cheltenham bungalow on a disability pension ever since," she explained to Kick one day, after team meeting in the break room.

Kick inherited this client from a PHN who was retiring and who prioritized her case load by making a pile of those who could be discharged and those who would benefit from ongoing follow-up. "You'll need to earn his trust," she told Kick. "But I know you're just the right fit for him. Go slowly and follow his cues. Tell him I wish him all the best."

Today, Kick was visiting Mr. Morris for the third time, so she knew to slow down as she approached the sloped, majestic badlands—not like the first time, when she felt her car go airborne. Her stomach hit the floor as she gripped the steering wheel for dear life; then she slowed her car down enough to be able to take in the beauty that was to her left. *What is it about this place?* she wondered. *It looks how Mars must look.* The good thing was this was the perfect entrée for an easy conversation with Mr. Morris, who was able to tell her all about it. With this topic as their starting point, he could advise *her* about speeding on Olde Base Line, as opposed to ending up in a one-sided, advice-giving session, with Kick's focus being the dangers of self-imposed exile on mental health and quality of life.

Today, Kick and Keith had agreed that they'd go over a folder of community services for fifty-five plus folks in Peel and talk about which, if any, appealed to Keith. Kick desperately wanted to help him out of his depression, for she understood that the longer he went without seeing others and doing things, the greater the likelihood that he'd never get past it. She had only recently begun to push, ever so slightly, knowing that an incremental excess would disavow her of the trust she sought to maintain. She was striking a careful balance informed by evidence-based knowledge of how trauma in men played out and the need voiced by many men to handle things *on their own.* She understood that this was code for not showing any weakness. Ever.

"There's a lunchtime soup kitchen the west side of Orangeville that needs volunteers," Kick told Keith.

"Uh huh."

"There's the fifty-five plus club in Inglewood."

He grimaced, slightly curling his lip.

"Oh, there's the Caledon Animal Shelter. They need people to play with the cats and walk the dogs."

His eyes softened. Kick held her breath. He reached for that pamphlet. "You mean, uh, you mean to pick them up and pet them?"

"I think so. The staff can't do it all day and apparently there's a real need to keep them company while they wait for their forever homes."

Mr. Morris smiled, continuing to read the pamphlet. Kick thought this might just be it. "I mean, there's a little screening process I'm sure, but then …" Startled, he looked up at his nurse with fear in his eyes.

"What if they recognize me? Nope. Not doing it." He got up, tucked his shirt tightly into his pants.

"What do you mean?" Kick asked.

"As the driver. You think everyone's forgot? No chance of that. Sorry, Kick. No can do."

"Mr. Morris. Keith. Please, can we talk about this? Of course, you have every right to choose what you will and won't do, but please let me help. What happened that day was a horrible, devastating accident. I can't even imagine what it was like for you. You've held onto this for so long. I promise to just listen."

Kick was doing what her training prepared her for: to transparently care, offer herself as a vehicle, and facilitate healing on the terms of her patients. The proverbial ball was in his court. She made no secret of her wish that he'd choose to answer her invitation to embrace his vulnerability by telling her his story. And finally, today, he did. He shared every detail and as he did, they shared a solemn space of grief, with both crying quietly at different times. He allowed her to touch his hand—the same hand that gripped his rig's large steering wheel as he attempted to avoid hitting someone's daughter, someone's son.

After he finished, he let out a large sigh. Keith asked, "Would you like a cup of tea? I sure need one."

Kick had another appointment, but this was far too important to abbreviate. "Yes, I do, thank you. I just need to grab something from my car."

"Do you like gingersnaps?"

"Of course! Who doesn't?"

Kick went to her car and called the office, asking them to notify her next client that she'd come at four o'clock, rather than one. She knew it would be okay; this particular client was always home at four, because *General Hospital* was on at three. She never missed her show.

Over tea, Kick tried to reduce the vulnerability her dear patient must have been feeling. Uncomfortable for many, but for Keith, it was nearly unbearable. How Kick wished more was done for boys and men to enable them to feel and express a full range of emotions. Much of her work in the schools surrounding mental health was related to societal expectations and countering them. So many times, when she was to see a young man for mental health concerns, he had bottled everything up for so long that the core wound was irretrievable.

"Thank you Kick. I'm sorry. I'm so, well ... I'm just sorry."

"There's nothing to be sorry about. What happened to you was and is a huge trauma. You lost so much, too. It is not dissimilar to the experience of a Toronto subway driver when a passenger falls, or worse. Or the experiences of first responders and what they see and endure."

Just then, the thought occurred to Kick that maybe if Keith were to volunteer with fire fighters or first responders, he'd find a kindred spirit of sorts. *To be continued ...* she thought.

She thanked her patient for the tea and drove to a quiet spot to take her (now late) lunch before heading over to see her next client: Miss Josephine Fraser.

Even in a garden smock, Jo looks smart. Just a bit of eyeliner, a hint of lipstick (always pale pink), and her thinning white hair pulled back in a French roll, held in place with two tortoise-colored pins. She walks with an enormous limp, but never let that keep her from doing the things she loved: cooking, preserving, drying herbs, gardening, and, of course, hosting. And by the end of today, she'd have done all five.

Josephine Fraser's board and batten house is set back a bit back from the main road, halfway up the hill towards the schoolhouse and the grocery store. Her huge front porch is adorned with two rockers and white wicker tables beautified with fresh flowers from her garden. Out back is a small but adequate covered porch with three steps down to her tidy backyard, potting shed, and large herb and vegetable garden. Along the shady side of the house is a manicured shade garden with lovely Hosta, Periwinkle, and Lily of the Valley.

Besides gardening—and, of course, preserving what she grows—Jo loves to have company. Her mother taught her everything she knows about hosting luncheons, teas, and dinners, and Jo spares no effort in making sure everyone feels special when they come over. One group in particular has been meeting at Jo's house for years: The Paisley • Corners Women's Institute. "The Institute," as it's generally called, has been meeting in kitchens, parlours, and backyard gazebos for as long as Paisley • Corners has been around. Longer, probably. Before that, this hamlet that Jo calls home was known as Tarbox Corners, but don't mention that around Mabel Tarbox or she might just have herself a conniption fit. Mabel will tell you that her husband's family founded this hamlet and when its name was changed, many Tarboxes moved away in protest. Some got mad. Some got married. Mabel got busy. She channeled her frustration into productivity and has been leading local groups and committees ever since. She runs her various committees and causes much like she ran her one-room schoolhouse up on the top of the Paisley • Corners hill. Organized. Structured. Kind. Productive. And welcoming.

Josephine Fraser was named by her pa, much to the chagrin of her delicate mother, Rose. Ezekiel Fraser was a brawny railway man whose claim to fame was having worked on the section of the Canadian National Railway that used to run through Paisley • Corners. And it was *his* grandfather who was *the guy* who set the CN railway's last spike in 1885 in Craigellachie, British Columbia – something he was proud of, "big time!" But you see, big Zeke had a big secret. No, it's not that he drank, or played the ponies in the Big Smoke (as Toronto was called when he was growing up), or even that he used to be a Methodist (God forbid). Zeke Fraser secretly loved a "girls'" book. That's right: six-foot, plaid-wearing bearded Zeke Fraser loved and read a book he kept hidden in his old baseball mitt—he'd read it over sixty times! —and only Rose and Zeke's own mother knew it. It was his love for this book that gave way to the name he gave his baby girl.

Barely a day after Josephine was born, Rose staged a sit-down strike (as soon as she *could* sit, that is) in protest of her husband's inflexible demand for her baby girl to be named Josephine Rose. "You'll call her Jo, just like that tomboy in *Little Women*. I know it. I just know it. And no proper Christian daughter of mine will be named a boy's name. Nicknames be damned!" Jo's mother *never* swore, and she almost fainted hearing her own mouth utter such words. At least, that's the way Jo tells the story whenever she's asked about her name by newcomers to Women's Institute picnics, rummage sales, church teas, and the like.

Jo was always an unconventional type, wanting to wear pants when females just didn't, tobogganing on a shovel with the boys down the Alton Pinnacle, and playing pond hockey behind the Cheltenham General Store. Born of quintessentially gendered parents—a mother who never left the house without lipstick, gloves and a hat, and a father who would turn his underwear inside out to get the most wear out of them (why waste laundry soap or well water?) —Jo seemed destined to bypass these confines. Maybe her name did that for her. Maybe, in some way, being called Jo gave way to a blending of all things good about both her parents. She was excellent at math, or, I guess you'd call it arithmetic in those days, and since this was something just not typical for girls, she was, by some, considered strange. "Piss on 'em all," her dad would tell her. "Pray for their souls," her mother would counter.

Jo also excelled at languages, literature, woodworking, and gym. But mostly, she longed to study the stars. An avid cook, gardener, and quilter, Jo could also be found alongside her dad on weekends mending fences on the farm or hauling manure when her dad's back was sore. Zeke used to brag to anyone who'd listen that his Jo was able to throw a baseball as hard as the boys, and then "on the turn of a dime, clean up, and be right ladylike."

When other girls were concerning themselves with the new hair ribbon colors at Burrell's General Store, Jo could most often be found at the Badlands, hiking and playing explorer with her best friend in the world, John Charles MacDonald the second. Everyone called him Charlie, rather than John or even JC, out of respect for JC the first—Charlie's dad was a decorated war veteran and a leader in Cheltenham, and everyone looked up to him. From April to early December, Jo and Charlie could be found outside throwing the baseball, in a tree house, or playing explorer on the Cheltenham Badlands. The exposed and eroded Queenston shale of the Badlands, with its reddish pink hues, was a draw to adventuresome kids who knew those rocks like the back of their hands: the slippery spots during the rain, the good spots to rest a can of grape Fanta, and the level spots to lay back and look up at the clouds and stars.

Jo and Charlie did almost everything together. They even called each other over to do their chores. When Jo had to put her laundry away, she'd call Charlie and they'd turn off the lights in her room and have sock fights. She'd divide up all her socks, being sure that each of them got one of the two long softball socks (they were the best for humming across the room at the other guy), and they'd see how many times they could pick each other off in the dim afternoon light seeping through her pulled blind. When Jo had the flu, Charlie held her hair back when she puked. Similarly, when Charlie took it upon himself to take some of his mother's Du Maurier cigarettes and smoked five of them in a row while walking home from their tree house, it was Jo who covered for him while he puked in the upstairs bathroom.

Yep, those two did everything together—well at least until Jo went away to school, and Charlie's mom died. Everything changed for Jo and Charlie when she went away to school, but after Charlie's mom died, life as he knew it changed for Charlie the most. Fact is, after Mrs. MacDonald passed away, no one in Cheltenham remembers seeing JC senior or junior again.

Even though Jo was such an unconventional girl in many respects, it was nursing school that called to her. From very young, Jo had a keen sense of the value in helping others, righting wrongs, and making sure everyone felt that they were important and deserved to be healthy. She visited Charlie's mom in the hospital several times, always fascinated by what the nurses were doing, saying, and writing down.

Right around her eighteenth birthday, Jo left country living for the "big city" and nurse's training at the Mack Training School for Nurses in St. Catharines, Ontario—a very prestigious nursing school indeed! Jo's mother developed dyspepsia at the very thought of her girl going so far away, despite the Mack School being known for its strong ties to the Nightingale System, which emphasized training nurses on knowledge of hygiene and medicine. But with the support of her father, Jo's mother finally relented to Jo going, much to her daughter's deep gratitude.

Nursing school proved difficult for Jo from the get-go. When she discovered that the school motto was *Video et Taceo—I see, and I am silent*—she just couldn't conceal her displeasure. In the first few weeks of the program, her instructor showed the class what they were working towards: their caps, the black band, and, of course, the certificate. Portrayed on this certificate was a candle holder in the form of a cherub with his fingers to his lips! Staying quiet was not Jo's strong suit and for the life of her, she couldn't understand how a nurse would be expected to observe yet be silent.

Jo loved most things about nursing school, but it was learning new things and accomplishing bigger and harder goals that propelled her into each new semester. She loved the placements, she loved her patients, and she just loved her uniform: navy and white striped fabric, crisp of course, with a bib apron. Hair off the face and up in some sort of style—this was the beginning of Jo's famous French twist.

With each placement and almost each shift, Jo saw something that needed improving, or changing, or worse yet, an injustice to address! "If girls could be lawyers, I swear, I'd be marching you down there myself to sign you up!" her favorite nursing teacher, Miss Helen Brown, once told her. Fondly known as "Brownie," Miss B. stood by Jo as countless doctors and nursing teachers sought to get her expelled for not following the expected rules for proper young ladies. And it was Brownie herself who put the black band on Jo's cap—a moment that Jo has never forgotten. To this day, atop her piano is the picture of Miss Brown and Jo as she received her diploma, pin, and cap.

Once the student nurses completed their training, they were able to choose from three options: private duty nursing, hospital and ward nursing, and public health. Jo chose public health, deciding to intern with a Red Cross outpost nurse in Big River, Saskatchewan.

Her mentor was Nurse Cobb—Eloise Cobb—a decisive woman with a firm jaw and etched lines on her face. Deceptively stern, she was more alike than unlike Jo, with decades of experience working in the most remote regions of Canada without a doctor for miles. A nurse-in-charge managed each hospital and lived in the community full-time. With the nearest doctor at least thirty miles away, it was the nurse who administered meds, set bones, treated fevers, delivered babies, gave vaccinations, and stitched wounds. Forced by circumstance, outpost nurses worked outside the boundaries of the typical scope of nursing practice. Jo loved that it was the Red Cross that sponsored the post and admired the flag, writing about its pridefulness in her letters home. She loved the autonomy and the problem-solving required for such a position. After six months, the position was offered to her full time, and she accepted it nearly as fast as she wrote the letter home to her parents saying so.

Jo spent five years as an outpost nurse, coming back home twice a year at Christmas and during black fly season in the summer months. She mentored new grads, ate meals with many a resident family, and she flourished, steadied by her firm rooting in the ethics put forth by Florence Nightingale herself.

When Jo returned home for the final time, it was because both of her parents' health was failing. She nursed them both and was the one who eventually called the travelling Caledon doctor for pain supports, when they each approached their final moments.

And so, Jo secured a job as a home health nurse in Caledon, and moved to Paisley • Corners, seeking a new start in the lovely board and batten house just outside the center of town. Despite working full time with the Victorian Order of Nurses, she quickly became involved in the Women's Institute as well as the Registered Nurses Association of Ontario, ascending rapidly to be its president for two consecutive terms. Jo worked tirelessly advocating for birth control for women, having seen what several children in rapid succession does to families spiritually, relationally, and of course, financially. "A woman should have a choice," she'd argue. "There's nothing sacrilegious about that."

Today, decades after settling in Paisley • Corners, Jo was off to Foodville to get a few more groceries for the Women's Institute meeting. Something was bothering her, niggling at her, yet she wasn't quite sure what it was. Fearing she'd forgotten something, or worse, someone, she reluctantly pressed on with her day. She was excited about today's meeting not only because Jo simply loves company and cooking, but also because there was going to be discussion about the commemorative plaque the Institute was sponsoring on the Caledon Trailway. The plaque would be dedicated to Jo's great grandfather for his role in setting the last spike of the CN railway. Jo wanted today to go "just right."

"Good morning my dear," Jo said to young Tanis. "Studying, I see?"

"Uh huh, always. Nursing school is tough," she asserted. "You just can't fall behind. Not for a minute."

"Oh, that I do understand my dear—I myself am a retired nurse."

"What university did you go to?" Tanis asked Jo as she checked her items through the check out.

"Oh, my dear, back in my day we didn't go to universities. There were training schools for nurses, and I went to the Mack School founded by Dr. Mack himself. He loved his nurses, that he did."

"*His* nurses?" Tanis asked bewildered.

"Well, not his, *per se*, but he took it upon himself to make sure the girls were trained up right and that the principles of medicine and hygiene were front and center."

"Uh huh," Tannis said with minimal interest. "That'll be $43.68. Do you need a carry-out?"

"Here you go my dear, and no I don't … but thanks, just the same. Good luck with your studies. I'm just down the road, if you ever need any help studying."

"Have a nice day." Once Jo left, Tanis rolled her eyes and shook her head, almost pitying the *old woman.*

As Jo pulled up to her driveway, she suddenly remembered what it was that had been niggling away at her earlier that day. It was the new public health nurse: she had scheduled a visit with Jo for today to go over some of her doctor's recommendations. She could see Kick now, standing at her front door.

"Hellooooo …" Jo called out melodically as she opened the trunk of her car. Kick turned around and waved kindly. "I'm so sorry," huffed Jo, "I knew I had forgotten something, but if I had known it was your visit, I'd never have gone off to get groceries."

Kick helped Jo in with her packages and sat herself down at the kitchen table, taking out the referral from Jo's doctor. "I've got some lovely scones and I'll put on a pot of tea for us," said Jo.

"Lovely, just lovely. Thank you," replied Kick.

Once settled in, Kick explained her role and the reason for her visit, ensuring that Jo understood that Kick's visits were never compulsory and always grounded in a collaborative approach to determining a patient's priorities. Of course, Jo didn't need such an explanation, but she politely listened, welcoming the professionalism of a kindred spirit. Kick always made sure to explain the role and the rights of her clients up-front at the start of any new nurse-patient relationship she strove to establish. To Kick, it didn't matter if she'd be visiting once or several times over several years. Setting the context, explaining the role, and ensuring that her patient's wishes and voice was central was as natural to Kick as breathing. She remembered studying how to fail epically in establishing trust in nursing school—a tongue-in-cheek lesson from one of her favorite nursing professors. She never forgot just how awful the nurse was in the roleplay, and she made sure never to assume such a dominant approach in any of her interactions.

"As you know from our phone call late last week, your family doctor asked us to come to see you to assess how you are getting along here on your own with your … is it the left hip? And he's concerned about mobility issues? As well, he was wondering if you might have questions about hip surgery, rehab, and any residual impacts. Would it be okay if we discussed these things, or were there other things that you'd prefer to discuss, or not?"

"Yes, all that is just fine," replied Jo. "I know my doctor really wants me to get this hip surgery. He's been with me for decades; I'm sure he's noticed how I limp and he's just wanting me to have a good life. I just can't find a good month where I don't have anything booked, that's all!" Jo pulled out the milk calendar again and started to shuffle through it.

"It's never convenient to have orthopedic surgery because there is down time, and there is a need to bring in supports or go to a rehab facility for a while." Kick went on to describe the experiences of her previous patients, being careful not to share any information that would inadvertently breach confidentiality. Everyone knows everyone in Paisley • Corners, so Kick described situations from folks prior to her coming to the village.

Slowly, Jo's shoulders relaxed and she listened more and more, especially when options were laid out and improvements were described. "So, do you think I should do it?" Jo asked.

"Well, for sure this is a decision that you need to make for yourself, but what I can do is find out as much about the surgery, what to expect in the hospital, and the post-op resources available for you, whether at home or in the aftercare rehab centre. Then once you are sure you have all the information, you can decide. You might want to consider just booking the surgery so you have a date saved—and you can change your mind otherwise." Jo agreed, and Kick offered to let her family doctor know the outcome of their conversation.

Kick wanted to assess the safety of Jo's home, but to do so in a manner that was not intrusive. She asked for a tour of the unique home and saw multiple hazards around the house, including scatter rugs, no bars in the shower area, and broken steps leading to the garden. Appreciating that home visits have a distinctive tempo, with an intro, content, and wind-up, Kick decided that it really wasn't time to go over these concerns today.

"Well, I've taken enough of your time today, Miss Fraser."

"Call me Jo, my dear. Everyone does."

"I am around here later on in the week; maybe I could come by again and we can have a look at your garden?"

"Okay, my dear. You are a slick one—I know you probably want to see how I'm keeping, living here on my own, so sure, come back. Just let me know when."

Kick gently touched Jo's shoulder as she prepared to leave through the side door and smiled appreciatively. "You've got me figured out. Takes a nurse to know a nurse, that's for certain."

And with that, the two nurses, divided by decades but not by duty, parted ways.

CHAPTER SIX
MOORINGS

Munsie Feed-n-Farm Supply was rarely ever closed. Even when the closed/open sign was turned, folks in Paisley • Corners knew they could call Munsie and he or one of his sons would help out. The days were rare when Munsie himself wasn't around, but Abner Wilkes lived for them. Not because he didn't like his lifelong friend, but because he liked to be in charge at the feed supply. He knew a lot, but was rarely asked about anything if Munsie was around. Except by Munsie.

This was the one week a year when Wilkes was always in charge: the week the entire Munsie Clan went to their cottage in the Muskokas. Abner had a new shirt on, a fresh shave and haircut, and he'd even cleaned his nails. Deep in thought, he rectified the bills from the day's sales and looked over the inventory. "Damn kid can't write clear enough to save himself," he said, shaking his head over Jamie who he secretly loved like a son, as he triple-checked the list of deliveries on the docket for tomorrow. Sitting in Munsie's chair, he reached to turn the *We're Open* sign around when the small bell over the main door jingled.

"Hello? Is anyone here?" the stranger called out.

"Yup, 'round the corner ... over here."

"Oh, am I too late? I mean is it okay, sir, if I come in to talk, er, to discuss an opportunity I'd like to ..." Wilkes took one look at the tall young man, dressed in khakis and a buttoned-down golf shirt, with a movie-star haircut and smile to match, and he thought, *Now what do we have here?*

"You lost, son?"

"Uh, no, sir. I, I mean we moved into Paisley • Corners last week. We bought the Old McCarthy place. Seth's the name," the young man said, extending his hand and exposing a shiny big watch. "Seth Smythe."

"Wilkes. What can I get for ya?"

"Are you the owner?"

"No, I am *not* the owner. I'm in charge and as you can see, I have a lot to do. So how can I help? Ya say you've got a big opportunity, eh? Just exactly what might that mean?"

"Can I sit here?"

"S'pose so." Wilkes pushed the stool towards him.

"Well, Mr. Wilkes, I recently completed a Master's of Science in Agriculture at the University of Guelph and my thesis was on genetically modified fertilizers. I'm very concerned about ..."

"Just how old ya say youse is?" Abner interrupted.

"Uh, well, I didn't, exactly. I'm twenty-seven. I know I look young, but ..."

"Look, we've got fertilizer. Piles of it. And we don't need no more. I'm sorry, but monetically gentifying anything 'round here, well, it just won't fly son. We're common-sense folks with generations of good, solid know-how. I don't exactly know what you've been doing at that university, but folks around here could teach those professor-types a thing or two, sure's sure."

"I'm sorry; I didn't mean to imply anything."

"No bother."

With his eyes darting, and his mouth slightly askew, Seth offered "I didn't mean to offend, sir."

Forced to respond, "You say your name's Smythe?", Wilkes asked.

"Seth, actually."

"Right. Thanks for coming in. See you around the village."

"Maybe I'll come back when the owner's here?" Seth offered.

"Suit yourself," Wilkes grumbled, and Seth strode out with a wave. Abner was right pissed this young milk-fed toth thought his decision might be overruled.

It was Friday morning, so it was laundry day for Dot Pinkney. She set a schedule and she kept it. She began to sort her laundry while looking out her window, where she'd often watch her neighbours. "Morning Patsy," she heard a friendly voice, followed by a car door slamming shut. "Sorry I'm late. Our nurses' meeting went a bit late and then I had a meeting with Community Services." It was that new public health nurse with the *ridiculous name. Like a character in a Lucy Maud Montgomery novel,* Dotty thought to herself.

"Hmmmph. I wonder why Patsy needs to see a nurse?" Dotty mumbled to herself. She paused, still going through the pockets of her pending laundry, wondering how she could find out why the nurse was at her neighbor? Just then, in her second-best post office smock, she found that letter she had stuffed away the last time she subbed in for Mary.

Miss Langdon (formerly of Hertfordshire, UK)
General Post Office
Paisley-Corners, Ontario
Canada.

"Missed the dot," she grumbled to herself, and plunked the letter on her kitchen counter and grabbed a measuring cup, heading over to her neighbour's house. She knew the pretense would seem pretty obvious, but she didn't care. She rang the bell and Patsy's daughter answered the door.

"Hello Nadine. You are looking smart today. Lovely outfit. I wonder, is your mother around?"

"Yes, but she's with the health nurse. Can I help you?"

"The *public health nurse*? Is she okay?"

"Oh yes; Mom and I have been talking about Mom's options for safe retirement living if she ever wants to move, so Mrs. Cavendish brought over some literature for us to review."

"She's—she's moving?" Dotty asked, alarmed. She was older than Patsy and somehow, this made her fear how others might be viewing her, as an older woman living on her own. Dotty had a real talent for making just about everything somehow about her.

"Nothing yet, we're just looking at options. Did you need something, though? I see you brought over a measuring cup?"

"Uh, oh. Yes. Right. Sugar. I mean brown sugar. Would that be ok? I need one and three-quarters of a cup for zucchini bread; the zucchini is needing to be picked shortly."

"Okay, sure, come into the kitchen. Mom and the health nurse are out on the patio, so we won't disturb them."

Dotty returned home, brown sugar in tow, with a softened heart about public health nurses—or at least, this particular one even if her name *was* a bit odd. If her neighbour relied upon and trusted her, maybe she could too. She was terribly lonesome since her husband died, and the nurses who visited him when he was dying were typically kind.

Deep in thought, Dotty returned to her laundry plans. She continued to separate her whites from darks and started her first load. It had looked so nice outside when she saw her neighbour and the nurse visiting on their patio that she opted to do the same. As she stepped outside again, she grabbed the UK letter from the kitchen counter.

The stamp was of the Queen Mom—*so lovely*, Dotty thought. A loyal monarchist, she was.

Dear Miss Langdon,

Please do excuse the intrusion of my letter, sent from a name you surely do not recognize. But I do believe we are related: our mothers were sisters, making you and I cousins.

In 1942, under the direction of the British government, mothers were instructed to send their children off to Canada and elsewhere to protect them from the war. My father had family in Ireland, so we were sent there. But your mother made the difficult decision to send you to Canada, hoping to keep you safe. My mum kept in contact with her until she died of tuberculosis.

My own mum died recently, and when I went through her things, I found a manilla envelope with some of your mother's personal papers. In it was a letter from Barnardo's indicating their belief that you ended up in Caledon Ontario but without any other details.

My husband and I don't have any children and when I found myself alone, I decided to try to find you—my cousin. I would love to connect with you, to get to know you, and to share stories of our lives before we were apart. When last I saw you, I was seven and I think you were six.

I do apologize again for writing to you out of the blue. I dearly hope that this correspondence does not bring you any grief. Please do contact me—my address and

telephone number are below. I also have included my
email address if that is helpful.

Yours most sincerely,

Abigail Cresthaven

Kick's day had thankfully slowed after a rough morning with a sick Alpaca. At dusk the day before, one of her alpacas, Nutmeg, couldn't get up. Together, she and Caleb propped him up and helped him into the barn. Down he went again. Giving him some time in case he was in pain, they waited a bit before getting him into his stall.

The next morning, Kick couldn't sleep, so got up and made coffee, thinking, hoping. She didn't want to awaken the barn too early, but when she couldn't wait any more, she walked across the driveway at five a.m. Normally, when she turned on the barn lights and brought in food dishes for the pig, duck, and chickens, several alpaca heads would pop up and glance over at her with their long eyelashes and glassy eyes. This morning, only two alpacas peeped over. Her stomach sank. She fed everyone and let the animals out of their stall to the hay that had been laid out the night before. Nutmeg stayed laying down, not moving. He was gone.

It appeared to have just happened. *How would the others cope*, she immediately worried. Alpacas are a communal species, always looking out for one another.

What had Kick missed? Should they have called the vet last night? With all the joy a small rescue farm brings, Kick's father had warned her, his soft-hearted daughter, that there would be much loss. While happy for her and Caleb that they had established a small rescue farm, he worried for her, knowing she'd take each loss rather hard. More loss she did not need.

After such a trying morning, today she gave herself permission to take an actual coffee break after her morning visit with Cormack Patterson—and to take it at a coffee shop. She and Mr. Patterson had met away from his house in order for him to discuss his wife's declining cognitive capacity. "I don't want to give up on her, but I'm getting worried about her safety. Our safety. If I talk about this in front of her when she's more with it, it'll kill her. If I talk about it when she's in a decline phase, well, let's just say that either way, it needs to be processed away from her."

"I feel like I'm being disloyal to her. I feel guilty. Like a bad husband."

Kick understood, having only recently attended a workshop on working with families affected by Alzheimer's. It can ruin marriages and creates all sorts of emotional upheaval, she recalled hearing. In her nurse's mind, she knew he needed to talk out loud. He needed to say what was on his heart. He needed to hear himself say the things he'd been thinking. At an appropriate pause, Kick quietly reassured Cormack that everything he was feeling was normal. She handed him a pamphlet from the Alzheimer's Society about the impact on families and the various options for care.

"You'll see yourself in some of the points made in this pamphlet," she told him. "This is a complete upheaval. Sometimes she's there, when other times, she's not. Coping is all about exactly what you are doing. First, processing how you are feeling, which I hope we are doing right now. Then learn of the various options, which we can go over today if the coffee shop stays quiet. Then wait for an opportunity when your wife is clear-thinking to discuss things. Most of the time, at least early on, the person knows things are changing. My guess is that Olive has some knowledge of her cognitive decline. She might even bring things up to you, relieved perhaps to finally say things out loud also."

The two went over the various scenarios, with none of them making Mr. Patterson any more reassured. What he was facing was a slow burn of loss: the painful witnessing of his wife remaining present in body but increasingly absent in mind.

"What I will say," Kick observed, "is that you need to have conversations now, while you still can. Say all you need to say. Bring up good memories. Take advantage of the good times. Live a full life. Do things. Go places. Have company. And for sure, you need to have supports in place for you. I can most certainly do that for you, but I also mean a family member or friend."

Mr. Patterson had grown increasingly somber. Kick knew he wasn't really hearing her at this point, and possibly missed a bit of what she had just said. She touched his hand, startling him out of his deep thought. "We'll go through this together. You're stuck with me. You're a good man and a loving husband. I'm just so sorry you and Olive are going through this."

Cormack opened his wallet and left fifteen dollars on the table. "Thank you, Kick. I'll see you next week, when you come to see Olive."

After Mr. Patterson left, glancing outside of the coffee shop, Kick thought she saw Old Joe. She got up, hoping to introduce herself to him. But just like that, he, whoever that was, was gone.

It was Old Joe. He had been trying to muster up the courage to go to Foodville, for he needed some provisions. But it was daytime, and he didn't have anyone looking out for him when he went to the grocery store. Not like before. No one like Loretta Putney. So, he'd wait.

Joe shuffled over to a bench and sat down, as his back was sore from the damp. He allowed his mind to float back to memories of Loretta's kindness from nearly a decade ago.

When Loretta was working at Foodville, Old Joe could count on a familiar routine. He would make his way from the ravine to the main road. Adjusting his Hudson's Bay coat and checking his pocket for his billfold, he'd mentally hope only *she* was working tonight. Beans, Weiners, Ovaltine, Bananas. Beans, Wieners, Ovaltine, Bananas. He'd lost his only pen and his notepads always got soaked through with dampness over time, so he'd remember his list this way.

Carefully pressed, she wore her Foodville smock well. Chatting with a customer while scanning items and placing them in bags, her nose would bristle: Aqua Velva. Her favorite customer had just come in. She would quickly tuck some day-old this-n-thats in a grocery bag and wait.

"How's doin, Joe? I'm so glad to see ya. Some thuderstorm t'other day." Joe would raise his eyes to hers, fleetingly holding her gaze.

"Sure was. Sure was."

"See that storm pipe swinging out over top of the window over there?" she motioned, pointing so he looked away as she placed the day-old items in his bag. "Sure could use your help to repair it."

Old Joe pays, and Loretta touches his shoulder as he passes her. "Tomorrow then?"

"Sure thing. Sure will."

He sorely missed Loretta. They both knew the dance, but they both participated. He offered his vulnerability to her, and she embraced and protected it. While he suppressed his shame, she worked diligently to suppress her pity.

Old Joe liked to think back about Loretta. It was a nice memory. Today, he decided his groceries could wait. The coffee shop looked busy and that meant that the grocery store was equally so. He made his way to the Caledon Trailway to take his "daily constitutional."

Kick left too. This was her afternoon at the high school, when the guidance counselor took appointments for her from noon until three-thirty. Kick loved working with young people and saw anywhere from three to seven students on her assigned day.

She pulled up and parked in the visitors' lot and made her way to the front office. She popped her head into the principal's office to say hello and let him know she was there. Her nurse's office was between the two vice-principals' offices—a move she didn't ask for, but one that the principal thought of in order to make her more visible to students at risk. Unfortunately, this arrangement didn't allow her the confidentiality of space her job required, especially in the eyes of students. They didn't want anyone to know they were seeing the nurse. So, she'd see teachers in that office and students in the tiny back office in the quiet Guidance department.

Today, the head of female Phys-Ed, Mrs. Carver, had booked in to see her. Kick loved their talks, as the teacher was a keen advocate for young women and embraced the role of the PHN in the schools. Kick taught often in Phys-Ed; sometimes the teacher left her on her own when the topic warranted only students and a nurse present. Today, the two planned out some teaching sessions. Then Mrs. Carver spoke with Kick about her worries about sexual health practices she was hearing about. After a frank discussion, the two planned additional curriculum and strategies for conversations should students come forward to the teacher again.

Kick then proceeded to Guidance to pick up her schedule, smiling at a nervous young woman thumbing mindlessly through a magazine in the waiting area.

"Kelsey, this is Miss Cavendish, the health nurse."

"Hi. Kelsey? Please call me Kick. I have a little office back here. Would that be okay?"

The young woman glanced down the hall; Kick noted her hesitation. "Where would you like to meet? Outside?" the girl nodded. "I'll follow you," Kick said with a smile.

The two sat on the bleachers beside the ball diamond. "I don't know where to start," Kelsey began.

"Well maybe let me tell you a bit about my role here at the school and maybe a bit about confidentiality and all of that." Kick proceeded to give her usual overview of the role of a PHN, focusing specifically on the many reasons that youth would see her and what they'd discuss in general. She explained her ethical duty to protect her patients' confidentiality and outlined the only reasons why she might need to contact a young person's family or someone in authority.

"But I'm not eighteen."

"Doesn't matter. You have a right to talk to a health professional. Even today, you can just get a feel of what it is like to sit with a school nurse. We don't have to get into any concerns you have unless you are in some sort of danger."

"No, nothing like that. What do some of the other girls talk to you about?"

Kick gave a few broad brushstroke descriptions of possible subject areas and asked her young hesitant client if she had any questions.

"Just one. Have you ever worked with 'a bulimic'?"

"Yes, I've worked with many young people with food and weight issues—Although I don't tend to like labels, they make people feel flawed, ill, and like they're to blame somehow. I used to do some work with NEDIC: The National Eating Disorder Information Centre. I loved it, even though I don't like that the word 'disorder' is in their name. Food issues stem from other issues. They are an outcome, not a disorder," the PHN explained. "Is this something you'd like to discuss?" Kick noted the reddened knuckles on Kelsey's right hand, characteristic of consistent self-purging.

"Sort of."

"Why don't you tell me a bit about what you already know? What your thoughts are about it, and if there's anything I might be able to clarify or elaborate upon?"

"Well, I know lots of girls do it. Some of them use laxatives. I'm just tired of it. It makes me feel worse, not better. Yesterday my heart was racing—I felt it sort of flutter." Her eyes dropped. Kick knew that her young client's vulnerability was out on full show, and that this moment and how she handled it, was crucial for earning trust.

"I bet you are. It's exhausting. So much gets bottled up, and sometimes the purging feels like a release, doesn't it?"

Kelsey nodded, now quietly wiping large tears from her cheeks.

"You obviously have given this much thought and you've made an appointment with a stranger to talk this out."

"I heard about you from one of my friends. She said you were nice and that you didn't judge."

"Well, that's good. One thing that I know helps me, is gathering a lot of information so I can feel a bit more in control. Should we do that and meet again?"

"Yes; when do you come to the school?"

"I normally come every Wednesday."

"Oh."

"I can come another day … When is your spare? We can meet on the bleachers again."

"My spare is always last class."

"Okay, how about I come in two days, and I'll meet you at two p.m. on these bleachers. Sound like a plan?"

Timidly, the girl agreed.

"Now, Kelsey, I always like to be transparent. No secrets. Normally I wouldn't even dream of telling someone I'd just met that I was worried about them or to ask them to make any changes in their health practices. But when you told me about your heart fluttering, I grew concerned. Just a bit. Would you be open to me telling you a little bit about why I'm concerned?"

"Yah, I guess so." The health nurse took care to explain the cardio-vascular impact of depleted potassium from chronic purging.

"Wow, I didn't know that. You must think awful of me."

"My goodness, no: I am concerned about your well-being. About you. You matter, Kelsey. You said you're tired of this. I bet you are. It is just exhausting – physically and mentally. Is it a frequent thing, or periodic?"

"Frequent."

"Would you consider, maybe, trying to purge just a bit less? And to avoid things that pull on your esophagus and are hard to purge?"

The health nurse was taking a harm reduction approach. She wasn't naïve enough to think that by the simple virtue of being her health nurse, that Kelsey would magically just stop, cold turkey. A harm reduction framework acknowledges this and encourages exactly what its name implies: reducing the harm.

Kelsey told her health nurse she thought she'd be able "reduce it down to half as much."

"Would you consider seeing your doctor, just to give your heart a quick check?"

"No, he'll tell my mom."

"What about the drop-in doctor, near the mall? They do not phone home."

"Ok Kick, if you think I should."

"I'm sorry Kelsey, normally I'm not this pushy. But your heart sent you a message. Maybe you knew this on some level, and that's why in part you came to see me. I'm just really proud of you. You really are practicing fantastic self-care. Shall I call and make the appointment, or do you want to? Did you want to go today?"

Kelsey agreed to walk over to the clinic herself, and the two of them booked another appointment on the school bleachers in two days' time. Kick waited until Kelsey was far in front of her before she went back into the school for her other appointments. The guidance counselor greeted her when she returned. "Thanks for seeing her, Kick. She seemed so scared. Is she going to be alright?"

Kick smiled. "I'm always happy to see anyone; you know that. I don't know what I'd do without you. You make them feel normal and not ashamed when they come to you asking to book an appointment with me. You are a big part of their journey, too. I'm so grateful."

Kick saw the rest of her young clients and made her way home, across the fifth line and down the main road to her farm and her animals and her life.

Kick took to her journal this evening—as she often does—to process the many things she witnesses and ponders.

Quite regularly, someone says to me, "Oh, but doesn't the farm and all those animals really tie you down?" Why yes, yes they do.

They tie me to starting my day when the sun rises and ending it well after the sun sets ... but this means I always get to see them both.

They tie me to the rhythm of the seasons ... the might of a winter's blizzard, the first spring breeze carrying the scent of rain, the majestic glory of a summer thunderstorm, and the fall of leaves from the poplar trees.

They tie me to the repetitiveness of farm chores ... a reprieve from yesterday's regrets or tomorrow's worries.

This farm and all these animals keep me tied down to earth when the rest of the universe tries to flip me upside-down.

I would much rather be tied down here than set adrift in the tumultuous sea where I see so many others floating. Lost. Unsure. Unsafe.

I find this mooring, and all of its predictability, rather to my liking.

CHAPTER SEVEN
SETH SMYTHE'S WORST SATURDAY

Seth Smythe had just graduated from the University of Guelph with a combined Bachelor's and Master's Degree in Agriculture. With his wife, Sinny, he recently moved into the old McCarthy farm outside of town. Both he and Sinny had quickly become a source of gossip and skepticism.

Today was no different as some of the regulars at Munsie's talked over the newcomers. "What in tarnation is a Bee Ag?" Abner Wilkes barked. Some of the men congregating near the coffee urn on the far side of the feed store nodded or smirked.

Cormack Patterson defended the couple. He'd met them months earlier in town and struck up a conversation with them both, intrigued with their academic background and achievements. He explained who Sinny was, telling the men a bit about her husband Seth and a bit more about university studies in agriculture. "Now, Abe, don't be so quick to judge. Some folks get their know-how through watching their families and learning from experience. Others, like this young man, go to university to learn. Why should we discourage it? I would wager he'd have much to teach us—probably as much as or more than we might teach him. Why not give him a chance?"

Wilkes shook his head. "I just don't get it. Like, who does he think he is, coming around here wanting to sell fertilizer to farmers who've been fertilizing Caledon for decades?" Others joined in, laughing and criticizing the gall of this newcomer.

Munsie glanced up at the clock and realized his meeting with the Equi-Grain rep was in five minutes. "Better end this tea party!" he announced. And with that, the men dispersed, some still laughing about Seth and the big idea he wanted to discuss.

Meticulous, scientific, eat-off-the-floor clean. Such was Seth Smyth's agricultural testing lab, which was housed inside his recently acquired barn.

Lights? Check
Bins closed? Check
Notes made? Check
Window open? Check.

But it was a particularly windy day in Paisley • Corners, and many farms, including Kick's, kept their chickens and other small creatures indoors. With one huge gust, the blunted two-by-four holding Seth's lab window open shifted and the window slammed shut. Seth looked up, startled. He had been finalizing his recently copyrighted Harvest App, which he hoped to talk about at a future Fall Fair. Based upon four years of rigorous science, with an intention to prevent lost harvests despite the fast-shifting weather changes due to global warming, the app was an open-access, free and multi-platform software aid. It had won an award and brought Seth much fame.

Unfortunately, it was within academe and government that the promise of the Harvest App was known, rather than among everyday farmers: Farmers who worked like Seth's grandfather had—the man who birthed his interest in agriculture. At one time in his life, his Pappy had lost not one, but two harvests in a row, and was forced to claim bankruptcy. Seth wanted to prevent this from ever again decimating a small farm. Seth set his sights on introducing his app to everyday farmers who were just like his Pappy.

For years Seth fine-tuned his Harvest App ©, most recently focusing on improving fertilizers that were not genetically modified and green. Now that he had his own lab, he could work on various iterations in order to finalize the best combination of ingredients for various crops. Above his workstation was the very first periodic table he'd ever owned, which his wife had laminated for him as a gift. Stored in his lab were the various ingredients he'd been experimenting with in his quest to come up with a better greener fertilizer. Seth wanted to spearhead a more organic approach to fertilizers—moving away from synthetic phosphates and the like. His lab had nitrogen, calcium, magnesium, sulfur, iron, chlorine, copper, manganese, zinc, molybdenum, and boron, to name just a few. Additionally, he was experimenting with lime and potash.

Today, Seth was working from an old formula, thought to be from Egyptian times, that involved adding the ashes from burned weeds to soil. He'd been gathering weeds from several areas of his property and had various piles, including black dog-strangling vine, bull thistle, Canada thistle, coltsfoot, dodder, and the largest Queen Anne's lace he'd ever seen.

"Do you want a coffee, Seth?" his wife asked him, popping her head into the lab.

"No, I'm fine. How are you feeling? Still nauseous?" Sinny was two months pregnant and was considered by some to be old for a first-time mother. Seth coddled her a bit, as they'd lost two pregnancies before this one.

Sinny ran her hand across her belly and shrugged. "I'm fine. I was sick only once this morning. That's progress, eh? Ok, I'll leave you to it. I'm going to do some shopping. I'll be back after lunch."

Seth began to gather the weeds; just outside the pull-up door of the barn, he set up a burning barrel where he was going to collect ashes for his fertilizer prototype. Slowly, he added the weeds, being sure to not add anything else in order to keep the ashes pure. One by one, he added different plants. He heard his cell phone ring and stepped back into the barn.

As Seth picked up his phone to answer it, the fire suddenly grew behind him. Within seconds, the Queens Anne's lace in the wheelbarrow beside the barrel caught fire. Seth panicked. He grabbed his new fire extinguisher and tried to put out the flames, but they continued to spread, catching the frayed rope of the pull up door. *The nitrogen! The sulphur!* Seth's panic rose as he called 911.

"This is Seth. Seth Smythe. I'm at the old McCarthy farm just outside of town. Do you know it?" The emergency dispatcher confirmed that she did, reassuring him help was on the way. "There's a fire, I … I tried to put it out, but it just keeps getting bigger. Oh God…."

After the reassuring voice on the other end of the phone told Seth to move away from the barn and settled him back into coherence, he managed to tell the dispatcher about the other items in his barn lab, including the chemicals. The first responders arrived with that knowledge in tow, but it was too late. The barn exploded as they pulled up, and they had a full-on, four-alarm fire on their hands.

The firefighters managed to save Seth and Sinny's adjacent house, but the barn burned down. Right down. Two firefighters were treated for chemical exposure and Seth was treated for shock.

Sinny, exhausted from shopping, arrived just after the last provincial police cruiser had pulled out. She could not believe her eyes. She found her husband safe but not sound: disheveled and dejected, he lay on their bed listlessly.

News travels pretty fast in small town Ontario, and Paisley • Corners was no different. The police cruisers, the fire trucks, the smell wafting in the air – all reasons for the men to congregate at Munsie's. In under an hour, they had a plan and everyone was on board.

Engulfed in shame and regret, Seth eventually dozed off with his wife's slender arms wrapped around him. As the sky darkened, a knock at their door startled them both. When Sinny went to answer it, she saw Cormack Patterson and Abner Wilkes standing on her front porch with sympathy in their eyes.

"Evening Mrs. Smythe. We met a while back. I'm Cormack Patterson, Olive's husband, and this is Abner Wilkes. Everyone heard about what happened today. Is your husband okay? How are you doing?"

"Oh, yes of course. Hi Cormack. We are okay, I guess. Still in shock. My husband wasn't hurt, luckily, but all of his work is gone ..."

Just then, Seth came to the door. The two local men reached out their hands, offering support the way many men do. Seth was surprised to see them. "Mr. Wilkes. Hello."

"Listen, son," Abner said, "we've got this. You'd be surprised just how many of us have had barns burn down. What happened for us, was when we were at our worst, everyone just showed up to help out. We'd like to make that happen for you, too. If you'll let us, that is."

Seth's eyes were bewildered. What was he hearing? "I don't understand."

Cormack smiled. "Well, it's simple, Seth. If you give us the okay, we'll have a team of men here in the next two days to clear away all that burned-up debris and then we'll build you a new barn. You just need to tell us what you need—size and features sort of thing—and we'll get on it."

Sinny and Seth looked at each other and then back at Abner and Cormack. They couldn't believe their ears. Seth's eyes began to fill up, with the tears being wiped away almost as fast as they arrived. Unreservedly, Sinny threw her arms around Cormack, kissing him on the cheek, gently.

"I'll make some tea," Sinny said, stepping back inside. Seth took Abner and Cormack around to the back porch, where the three men looked out over the burned grass and ashes.

Abner rubbed his chin. "I've got to ask, though. What in tarnation were you doing in there?"

Seth explained about his fertilizer experiments. Cormack listened. Abner shook his head, but Cormack quickly chastised him. "Now, Abe, now is not the time to ride the man. Let's get him a barn, and we can talk about everything else another time." With that, the men shook Seth's hand again.

"Your hand sure is sticky," Cormack noted, chuckling.

Seth looked at his palm. "The residue came off one of the weeds I was burning to make ashes to add to my soil. Sure was the biggest stalk of Queen Anne's lace I'd ever seen."

"Queen Anne's lace, you say?" Abner Wilkes asked. "Was it about yay tall and yay wide?" he said, motioning with his hands.

"Yes, really large. It had a sort of sap on it."

Abner's eyes widened. "Son, that's giant hogweed. It's toxic. And flammable! It's an invasive weed we've been battling in these parts for the last few years."

Mack could see that Abner was getting riled up, so he stepped in. "Well, now the boy knows. We've all got to start somewhere. Let's get this barn built and then why don't we all get together and we can listen to Seth's ideas? Maybe with all our heads together, we might come up with the next greatest fertilizer. Sound good?"

Seth agreed. Wilkes raised his eyebrows, opting not to commit. Sinny brought out some tea and sweets for the men to enjoy on the porch, and their conversation turned to items on town council, to crop shares and what else, taxes.

CHAPTER EiGHT
WHAT'S IN A SMELL?

It was a regular Tuesday morning in Paisley • Corners—except for the smell. On the way to open the barn and feed her rescues, Kick caught a whiff and worried something had died out on the main road. But after another whiff, she thought the smell seemed to be different from that, with fleeting hints of sulphur peppering the stench.

Wrinkling his nose in disgust at the scent, young Jamie from Munsie's caught wind of the smell while out with his deliveries, which always started with the outskirt farms like the Putney's, though he visited them less frequently now. Seemed he spent more time waving to folks in cars or on tractors than he did unloading his deliveries, that young Jamie. Such a pleasant and kindly young lad.

Since it was a Tuesday, Paisley • Corners' self-appointed matriarch and eventual secretary of every committee was already up and on her way. Even that smell didn't slow her down. Dotty Pinkney never slows down. She can't. Keeping up matters, tidiness counts, and order is compulsory. But her neatly pressed façade is like a summer peony. Behind the veneer of scented uniformity are disease-ridden ants, without whom the summer peony dies. "I bet I know where that smell is coming from," Dot murmured to herself as she crossed the light at the Three and a Half on her way to her weekly wash and set. *That vagrant's camp, probably*, she told herself.

Autumn in Paisley • Corners was generally damp or windy. Today was a bit of both and as the wind picked up speed, the smell travelled to every nook and cranny of the town. Up at Foodville, the manager was heard asking the new stock boys to check outside in case something got into the garbage dumpster. Over at the post office, Mrs. Offenbach asked everyone to "shut that door!", trying to keep the smell from coming in. At Bobby's Pin hair salon, Ginger sprayed Lysol near the vents, thinking something must have died in them and fearing her uppity customers from the new development would complain—or worse, just never come back.

The smell was disrupting *everything* in Paisley • Corners, and because of that, Kick notified the Environmental Health Inspectors' division of her public health unit. In the meantime, Theodore Buckett, head of the local provincial police division, decided to get to the bottom of things after being asked about the smell "some umpteen times." He opened up his cruiser windows and started driving in the direction of the smell—except that as the wind changed, so did the direction of the smell. He'd go east and then lose track … Then he'd stop, get out, and sniff, looking like a potbelly pig at suppertime. Then he'd go north, trying again to locate the exact source of the smell. "Dang it," he complained to himself as he stepped outside his car to catch the scent again, "It's like following a mole in the dead of winter!"

"Whatcha up to?" he heard someone say from a ways back. He turned around and there was Old Joe, known to the police as the harmless town vagrant, walking up from the ravine.

"Oh, morning. How's it going Joe?"

"Fair to middlin' ... fair to middlin'.'"

"You smell that? Geez—it seems to be coming from all directions. Ugh, it's the last thing I needed today. I've got a full docket at the courthouse to deal with. I've wasted so much time already, I just can't pinpoint where it is coming from ..."

Old Joe shuffled his feet. "It's comin' from the abandoned Tarbox well—I'm sure of it ... I walked up there earlier and the stench near enough knocked me over."

As Theodore Buckett looked Joe over and thought about this information, his cell phone rang—again.

"Buckett," he responded. "Who? Oh, right ... right. Well, funny you should ask. I think we might have located the smell. Do you want to meet me at the old well, say in five? Great. See you there."

And with that, the police officer set off to meet a team of health inspectors and investigate the well.

The closer Buckett got to Tarbox well, the worse the smell. Before getting out of his cruiser, he removed the wax paper in which he'd wrapped his egg salad sandwich earlier that morning, folded it neatly, and placed it over his mouth and nose.

Inspectors arrived on the scene just as he did and quickly made use of their equipment, sending down sample taking devices immediately. One inspector had what appeared to be a miniature lab in his trunk and he began to test the samples. Once they identified a few factors which they believed were causing the stench, they took more samples, including scrapings of the old, mottled stonework of the well itself.

"Do you know the year this well was built?" one of the inspectors asked Officer Buckett. "Eighteen-sixty or so."

The inspectors looked at each other and began to quietly discuss the age of the well and the findings in the sample. They agreed upon a plan of action. They called the local Works Department to bring a truck with a portable oxygen aerator. Within about twenty minutes, the truck arrived, and the first step of aerating the water and injecting oxygen commenced. They added chlorine, followed by hydrogen peroxide.

Slowly, the smell dissipated, but not the brewing controversy.

The remediation of the Tarbox well was big news in Paisley • Corners, and the story of the horrible smell made it to the front page of the paper. The chief health inspector, Officer Buckett, and a few of the town folk were all interviewed for the featured article. Beside it was a small piece on the history of the Tarbox well and its significance for the town during its early years.

The news coverage was meant to celebrate teamwork and the significance of the well, but members of the Revitalization Committee saw the well as another eye sore (well, nose sore) they needed to address. An urgent meeting of the Revitalization Committee's executive was held the next afternoon, with members voicing their concerns on a number of issues, including the Tarbox well posing a potential threat to the town's water supply (despite the fact that the well was not connected to any water supply and was spring fed).

Chiming in, two members indicated that on "several occasions" recently, when out for their power walks, they had smelled smoke, even though the fire department had issued a full fire ban. "It was coming from that hobo's squatter camp!" one of the executive members proclaimed. "It's not the first time, either. He's a tricky one though, he thinks he has outsmarted us, moving around and all. Nope. This was him alright. What's next? A grass fire that takes out a farm family's income? It's time we up our game!" Following discussion, the executive voted unanimously on two items:

Be it resolved that the PC Revitalization Committee petition the Planning and Development Committee to direct Town Works staff to fill in the Tarbox Well out of an abundance of concern for public safety; and

Be it resolved that the PC Revitalization Committee make a presentation to Town Council requesting an ordinance to remove any and all illegal encampments.

It didn't take long for the executive to bring their two resolutions to their main meeting, with both passing narrowly after moderate discussion on both sides. The Revitalization Committee were provided space to plead their case to the Paisley • Corners Town Council. Their first motion was defeated, following an impassioned counter-presentation by the Historical Society, who brought the chief public health inspector as their expert witness. However, Town Council passed the motion to "begin work to locate illegal encampments within and near Paisley • Corners."

Kick's work cell buzzed shortly thereafter, with the details of the meeting in her inbox. Some days, she wished she hadn't read her email. The news about municipal action against encampments, which clearly targeted Old Joe, had her questioning her community's sense of 'community.' The usually upbeat rural nurse and sanctuary keeper was growing weary, and she knew it. What could she do as a solitary PHN, given the arguments already made to Town Council and the outcome?

Kick recalled a similar council mandate in Toronto to move homeless persons out before the Pope arrived for a visit. Police and outreach workers were stuck with enforcing this ignominious act of overt exclusion. And when the Pope did arrive, where did he ask to go? To the so-called squatters' camps, the halfway houses, the shelters.

In her years as a nurse, Kick has honed a sense of when it is right to speak up, and when it is best to plant seeds of change, gently inviting shifts in perspective while opting to stay in the background. She's talked about this more than once with Jo Fraser, a kindred nursing spirit.

One morning not long after the town council resolution was passed, in the quiet just before the dawn, Kick took to her journal—a pensive repository for scattered thoughts in need of assembly.

> *I am tired. Tired of the utter disregard of people's life stories—the reasons, perhaps, that they end up in the situations they're in. Old Joe, Paisley • Corners' resident "vagrant"—as some of the otherwise kindly folks narrow-mindedly like to call him—is as much part of PC as anyone else. He's been here four times as long as me! He might have stains on his nineteen-seventies Hudson's Bay coat, but he brushes them off as best he can before he goes to the grocery store. He might have a scraggly greyed beard, but he shaves by Munsie's creek and puts on Aqua Velva before walking into the post office. And he may be of no fixed address, but he matters. Why his name became Item Three on the agenda of recent PC Revitalization Committee meetings cripples my spirit and saddens my nursing soul. But today, I will speak. I will invite those who have a home, have a bathroom sink, have a new winter coat, and who appear to have an un-shattered sense of dignity to pause and think on this one point. Who gets included in the proverbial "we" or "us" when it comes to PC? Joe matters. His life's longings do not become extinguished because he's dirty or old or homeless. He loves, has been loved and needs us, all of us to love him now. For how can a small Ontario rural hamlet prevail if not through the intentional inclusion and protection of all?*

Kick closed her journal and decided to email the Executive Director of Community Services, who had asked for her help regarding outreach to Caledon's most vulnerable. At the off-chance that he might be available the next day, Kick asked for a meeting over coffee.

To her delight, Kick awoke to an email from the ED offering to meet any time this morning—just to let him know where and when. He also asked to bring a community member and his key outreach worker. Kick checked her schedule and made the appointment for nine a.m.

When she entered the coffee shop at the appointed time, she saw Eli Zechman with a gentleman who could've been Old Joe's brother, he looked and dressed so similarly. Just behind her, a woman entered the shop, accidentally banging into Kick and knocking her folder to the ground.

"Oh my, sorry about that! I'm a bit late. I didn't see you there."

"It's okay, really." The two bent down to pick up papers. Just then, the woman saw Kick's name tag.

"You're who I'm meeting with, I think. I'm Lisa, the outreach worker. I work with Eli."

"So nice to meet you."

"I think I owe you a coffee, Ms. Cavendish."

After they ordered their coffees, Kick and Lisa approached the table where Eli and the other man were seated. "Eli, so nice to see you again," Kick said, reaching out her hand to shake his.

"Kick, good to see you. How's the farm?"

"Oh wonderful. Busy, but wonderful."

"I think you've already met Lisa, our senior outreach worker, but I'm not sure if you've met Dan. Dan is on our community advisory council and I thought he'd be perfect to join us this morning for our conversation."

"Dan, so good to meet you." Kick reached out her hand and shook his warmly. She sat down. "Well, I'll get right to things if that works," she began. "I'm not sure how busy you all are today. It's about the meeting at Town Council the other night. Did you know that—"

Dan interrupted. "You mean about the cops getting rid of encampments?"

"Uh, yes. Uh, oh, you know this? Yes, of course you know. I mean, well—yes, that meeting."

Dan nodded. "I was at that meeting. There wasn't time, or so they claimed, for any more community feedback by the time it was my turn to speak. Others spoke, but they were pretty much all in favour of the resolution. All of them were from some committee with a long name. Can't quite remember."

"Dan volunteered to represent our agency and attended the meeting last night. So we're well versed on this movement and this dreadful decision," Eli added.

Kick re-thought her approach. She knew better to ask what, if anything, was already going on regarding a given social issue. She regrouped and asked, "I'm a bit out of touch, perhaps. Can you tell me a bit about how Community Services is involved with this issue? Let's start there and I'll try to contain my dismay about the meeting," she admitted.

"Kick, your passion is one of the things we most admire about you," Eli said reassuringly. "Clearly you understand that this is a monumental decision with underlying assumptions about disadvantaged persons. That is why I approached you at the poverty network meeting a few weeks ago. Your email came at the most opportune time. I, too, was up late fretting about things. Lisa, why don't you and Dan talk a bit about what is going on?"

With that invitation, Lisa provided an overview of their outreach priorities and activities and Dan provided insights regarding his own lived experience of precarious housing and living rough in Caledon. Kick thanked them for the overview, making notes the entire time.

"I'm especially worried about a gentleman some of the residents in Paisley • Corners call Old Joe. When he finds out, about the resolution I mean, I fear he'll go underground, or worse, we'll lose him to Toronto."

Lisa and Dan nodded. "I can't say too much here, given confidentiality, but Kick, please trust me that we are on it," Lisa said.

Kick's shoulders softened and she let out a sigh. "I've been so worried but haven't wanted to push to see him. As you know, visits from a PHN are completely voluntary."

Dan reached across the table, "Miss ... I only wish there were more out there like you. We are also worried about the impact of this decision on lots of guys who are hiding in plain sight like Joe. We'll do everything we can."

Eli glanced at his watch. "So Kick, what I was hoping is that you might have the time and the interest to lead a community consultation and assessment regarding homelessness in Caledon, and—here's the kicker—we'd need it to be both thorough and fast, so we can try to counter this at Town Council."

Kick didn't need to think about it. In addition to home visits, PHNs often engage in community assessments and consultations, partnering with members of the community in order to collaboratively address key issues impacting health and quality of life. She agreed immediately, beginning to plan her community development strategies in her head. "Dan, would you work with me?" she asked. "I can come up with some preliminary questions to ask, but I'd prefer to vet them through you to ensure their appropriateness. Maybe you have some time this week?"

"I've got all morning," he replied.

"Me too," Lisa added.

"Great," Eli said, getting up from his chair. "I leave this with all of you. Kick. Dan. Thank you so much. Lisa, we'll touch base tomorrow morning then. Lunch is on me if you stay that long," Eli offered.

Together the PHN, the community member with lived experience, and a key informant mapped out a rapid response strategy aimed at consulting with the community in order to provide a starting picture or "snapshot" of the issue of Caledon-specific homelessness and precarious housing. Afterwards, Kick stayed back to write up some reflective notes and to make an important call.

"Keith? It's Kick. Kick Cavendish, your public health nurse."

"Hi, Kick. What's going on?"

"Keith, sorry to call out of the blue, but I wondered if you could help me."

"Sure—if I can, I mean."

"Keith, I need your help on a committee to look at folks who are homeless or on the brink in Caledon. I'm going to need a team to meet with various stakeholders, people in the know, family members and folks with direct experience. I sure could use your kind approach. What do you think? Maybe we could meet and talk about it?"

Mr. Morris hesitated. This time, this call from the public health nurse felt different. Better, somehow. This time, his nurse was asking *him* to help *her*. Her invitation leveled the field. She had hoped it would.

"Kick, I'm in. How can I help?" The two promised to meet. Kick told Keith she'd be in touch in the next few days, once the team met to finalize questions and the outreach workers had some time to connect with persons with lived experience.

"I'm expecting four people for my meeting," Kick told the receptionist at the health department. "I'll be just getting the space ready—the small meeting room with the windows."

Kick set out teacups and muffins and sorted through her notes one last time. How would she tell Eli that she didn't' think it was right to rush this process—that she'd barely be able to scratch the surface in her community consultation process if it needed to be done in three weeks? He was a social worker, after all, so well versed in community development principles and practices. Deep in thought, she didn't hear Keith Morris come in.

"Hey Kick, I'm here. You know, I have to say, helping you out with this process wasn't that bad after all."

"Oh, Keith. Wow. You're doing so great! I mean, well, you know."

"I just thought, 'Is this about me, or is this about those guys forced to live in their cars or in abandoned barns?' I had to get over myself and I promised I'd help you so, here I am."

"Just fabulous, Keith. Thank you so much." Kick introduced Keith to Dan as he walked in the door, and once Eli and Lisa arrived, everyone introduced themselves while Kick poured tea. Then she initiated their meeting.

"Thanks, everyone. I'm so glad we could meet sooner rather than later. I want to start by thanking Dan and Lisa for working so hard to get a list of stakeholders, key informants, and persons with lived experience together, so that we now have a beginning plan. We've got our general questions, we've got our goals in mind, and we now have Keith who will be helping us do the consultations. It's just that, well, I've really been troubled by the rush of the thing."

"Well, that's on them," Eli interjected. "They're the ones who are rushing the attack on the homeless, not us. We have to get some ammo to stop it."

"Yes," Kick replied, "I do hear that—it's just that, well, you know these sorts of things can't be rushed. Lisa and Dan have some rapport already there with many of the folks we'll be consulting, but we still need the time to work with these community members, process what we hear, and write it up in a way that honours what we've heard and presents a strategy to the town."

"Agreed", said Lisa, sheepishly smiling at Eli.

Kick continued. "So, what I was thinking we could do today is fill out an application for an injunction of that Town Council motion to buy us some time. The maximum we can get, apparently, is a ninety-day hold on it to provide us time to gather information and come up with a strategy." The group of five discussed the pros and cons of Kick's suggestion, eventually agreeing to apply for the injunction. Just then, Kick's cell phone rang, and she excused herself from the group.

"Yes, this is she. Yes, that's right, we were hoping to present our rationale for an injunction at the next possible opportunity. Uh huh. Right ..." Kick glanced at the group, pointing frantically at her phone smiling. "Today? Uh, can you hold for just one moment?" Kick put her phone on mute and turned to her group, her mouth now dry.

"They have a cancellation today. They said if we could come and present at six-thirty p.m. today, they'd hear our request for an injunction."

"We're not even really ready," Lisa admitted.

"Let's do it. I'll speak, if you want me to," Dan added.

"Eli?"

"I've got the board meeting tonight. Lisa, do you think you can clear your schedule?"

"Yes, I can for sure. Kick, do you think you'd be able to come?"

"I have a visit, but I can make it a dinner time visit. She'd like that, my client, I think. I would just head over to the council chambers afterwards."

"I'll come just to listen and learn," Keith said.

Kick unmuted her phone. "Hello, sorry about that. Our group was actually just meeting. We'd be so pleased to come today. Thank you for this opportunity. Truly." Kick worked out the details with the Town's representative and the group got down to work, immediately strategizing how they'd back up their request for an injunction, what they'd plan to produce, and most importantly, take the time to explain the problems with a mandate to remove vulnerable persons from Caledon—from anywhere. They knew they had their work cut out for them, but passion and compassion were on their side. They knew the facts and they had lived experience to draw from. And they had a solid plan to conduct a full community consultation and provide a report.

At the Town Council meeting that evening, Lisa provided statistics about precarious housing in Caledon and of the kinds of client needs that their community services provided. Kick provided a national picture of the kinds of community programming and policies that were harmful or were helpful. She suggested the establishment of a nurse outreach team, providing examples from Barrie, North Bay, Guelph, Shelburne and Peterborough.

But it was Dan who held the focus of the mayor and councilors as he shared his own story of "living rough," as he called it. He talked about a series of losses and of the increasing stigma he faced with every unravelling thread disconnecting him from mainstream society. He talked about what he needed and what he didn't. He confronted myths that blame folks for their circumstances. He told them what had made a difference for him and what he believed other folks living rough would want in the name of help or support. Most importantly, he warned of the devastating impact of police being mandated to remove encampments. "Everything I owned, I carried in one hiker's backpack. To others, it was filth. Garbage. To me, it was the last remaining remnants of my self-worth—proof that I used to matter."

Throughout the proceedings, Keith looked on, listening to his peers while reflecting in bewilderment at how he had pushed himself to "get over himself," as he'd say. He felt hopeful. Maybe, in some way, he hoped to atone for the accident. He was out, engaging, and leaving his life of self-imposed exile in the past.

After the earnest group of five was done presenting, the mayor addressed them. "I want to thank you all for coming on such short notice," he said. "We don't often see you public health nurses, Ms. Cavendish. We know you're there, but it's good to hear you speak. Lisa, thank you as always for all you all do in Caledon. Dan—may I call you Dan? Thank you. I think I can speak on everyone's behalf to say you have really touched our hearts with your honest testimony tonight. They are very lucky to have you on this committee, doing what you do and providing all of your experience and guidance.

"We will take your application tonight for an injunction very seriously and we will be in touch as quickly as we can with our decision."

The group of five stayed in the dimly lit parking lot of the town council hall long after they'd left the meeting. Dan was telling stories from the street, as he called them, and everyone was laughing along with his jokes. Even Keith was laughing, with Kick smiling warmly at him, and he understood why. A back door of the hall opened and one of the councilors exited, making his way over to the group.

"Councilor Stokes. Thanks again for letting us speak," Kick said appreciatively.

"It's been a long night, but everyone wanted to stay and discuss your presentation. You'll get a formal notification tomorrow when the clerk types it up, but council voted unanimously to approve your request for an injunction and rather than ninety days, we've granted one hundred and eighty days. In the notice you'll receive will be a due date for your report and proposal. You'll be invited to present again to council in six months. How does that sound?"

Bleary eyed, Kick reached out her hand to the councilor, thanking him on behalf of the group.

Driving up the road to her farm, Kick knew that while this was a victory of sorts, her group would have their work cut out for them. Stopping the dismantling of encampments for now was great. But to change attitudes grounded in victim-blaming— that takes time. That takes community engagement. And that takes a measured balance between patience and diligence. Good thing public health nurses have all of that in their proverbial toolbelt.

CHAPTER NiNE
FROM AWAY

Dotty Pinkney looked forward to the *Caledon Times* newspaper every Thursday. Often, her photos were featured as part of the reporting on various events in the village. This Thursday, she poured an Earl Gray tea, as she did most evenings, and started in. Thumbing, reading, making notes on trunk sales or deaths or town council decisions. She thought of the photo of the Tarbox well she had provided to the paper, along with a one-page history of it, for the issue that came out after the incident of that terrible stench. History matters. That well had served the hamlet for decades. It deserved to survive. *One less fight for the Historical Society*, she thought.

She had been equally pleased with the announcement that Town Council had passed a motion to eliminate illegal encampments within and near Paisley • Corners. *Long overdue*, she thought. It had been thanks to a phone call with a member of the Revitalization Committee executive that Dot had the gumption to push for this move weeks ago.

"We will never be able to measure up if we don't change things around here," she had told her friend over the phone that day. "For four months now, we've still not discussed Old Joe, the embarrassment of Paisley • Corners. I don't know why he stays or why he can't just clean himself up a bit. How hard can it be to get a coat? There's a thrift shop just in the next village. And a razor, I mean, come on! Clean up your act. But then again, why would he? They're all the same. Too lazy to get a job and living off the good will of others. I'll be damned if I let those do-gooders keep putting off talking about him at the Town Council meeting tonight. All we talk about is sidewalks, flower boxes at the centre of town, and how to maintain the quaintness of our historic village. That's not revitalization. It's same old, same old. We'll never measure up. And, we won't attract new business or commerce or growth here. It's the ne'er-do-wells like Old Joe who're keeping PC back and no amount of windowsill paint, village flower beds, or flags on Canada day will change what a sighting of our village vagrant will do. He needs to go and tonight, I'm moving it to Item One." And with that, she had bid her friend and comrade in perspective a good day and placed a very warm telephone receiver in its cradle. Later that evening, the town council was powerfully swayed to move to action, and recalling the news coverage the next day gave Dot a smug sense of self pride.

And then …..

Jarred back to the present by a headline in her paper, her mood suddenly changed …

PRIME MINISTER to apologize for the Canadian Government's role in the mis-treatment of British Home Children.

Within moments, Dotty's collar was drenched and her mouth went dry as she read about the "frightened youngsters sent to Canada," called "degenerates" at the time by Prime Minister Diefenbaker in the House of Commons.

> *Mass Grave in Park Lawn Cemetery ... Few permitted*
> *to go to school ... Many died of preventable disease,*
> *abuse and neglect ...*

Dread enveloped her. Fear engulfed her. Struggling to get up, sweaty, yet cold, Dot worked her way to her closet. On all fours, she pushed aside assorted luggage, boxes, and bins. And there, in the furthest recessed corner was a trunk—a memory-laden, labelled trunk of hidden histories and forgotten family. Barnardos.

The following day, Old Joe was just finishing up his rounds, checking on shut ins, delivering firewood to back porches, and looking out for 'his' turkeys after a full moon's exposure of their hiding spots. Some would say Old Joe had no friends, that he was a loner. But Old Joe found friends in the crows and in the forgotten small animals once the delight of children long since grown. He knows the squirrels, the chipmunks, and yep, even the weaselly weasels— brown in summer, white in winter. He's become one with the land, with Caledon and her bounty in the fall, and her winds of the spring. He can read the sky ... can smell the onset of rain ... and has cleared branches near hydro lines ahead of many seasons of winter ice. Today, on his way home, he found a copy of a recent paper, walked it down to his camp, made some coffee, and sat in his chair, intending to read it cover to post.

With a narrow margin, Town Council passed a motion sanctioning the Caledon OPP to take any and all measures required in order to eliminate illegal encampments within and near Paisley • Corners.

Joe frantically looked at his home, realizing he'd have to pack up, and pack up now. The police might arrive at any moment to take away his belongings and put him who knows where.

In the rush, he tripped and fell on a folded left wrist. The pain made him nauseous, but he couldn't stop. Not now.

Plus, it had rained the night before. He remembered something his dad, who worked for the RCMP, had once told him. "Mud never lies," he'd told his son, in reference to his work tracking down the bad guys. Undisturbed, it reveals the passings by, the journeys made. *They'll see my footprints*, he thought. He'd been up and down the ravine a few times, creating the distinctive path of an elderly man's boot marks. In his head, all he could hear was "Mud never lies. Mud never lies."

He knew his life was a lie. His camp was his punishment. And now, it was going to come all crashing down.

Weeks passed after that newspaper article and no-one saw Dotty. She missed her shift at the post office. She missed her weekly wash and set. She missed meetings of the church women. And when she missed her B12 injection with the nurse practitioner, her family doctor's office called the public health department and requested a well-elderly visit. Kick took the referral. She went to Dot Pinkney's home right away.

"Dotty? Dot? It's Kick—the public health nurse. Are you up?" Slowly, as the locks clicked, slid, and unhooked, a gumption-less woman greeted the Paisley • Corners Public Health Nurse.

"Now everyone will know," she murmured to herself, seeing Kick on her porch.

Slowly, Kick passed through the darkened entrée to a motionless house, seemingly stalled in a moment of time. "I've been calling, Dotty, but when I couldn't get a hold of you, I thought I'd drop over. I'm dearly sorry for the suddenness of this. Must feel like an intrusion."

Dotty sat down in the kitchen, trying to adjust her housecoat to cover her nightgown, threadbare and stained.

Kick followed her lead and pulled out a chair, moving papers and envelopes to one side. In front of her was a shadowy rendering of the woman Kick had come to know through visits to the post office, Town Council meetings, and the other opportunities where Dotty was known to assert herself and her viewpoints. But this morning, sat an etched version of a woman once robust: a vulnerable state deserving of compassionate protection.

"Dotty, can I make us a cup of tea? Or coffee?" Seeing the dryness of her patient's mouth and her weakened state, Kick asked if she might make herself a piece of toast also. "Your doctor wanted me to drop by to see how you are. She's worried about you."

"I'm fine," asserted Dot.

"You seem down, Dotty. You also appear rather weak, and I wonder if something has happened. I don't want to pry, but you know us nurses. Always asking questions," Kick offered, only half-jokingly.

After a few minutes of puttering at the kitchen counter, Kick sat down with two plates and two pieces of buttered toast. The jam was already on the table and she helped herself, then passing it to Dotty, hoping she'd add some. "What kind of tea is this? It's lovely"

"Typhoo. It's British naval tea." Kick was relieved she had gotten more than a one-word answer. *Progress sometimes comes in bits and spurts. I'll take it*, she thought.

"Well, I'll have to try to get some. I'm not sure where I'd ..."

Dot interrupted her. "You can get it here in town or in Orangeville, too. It's pretty popular. I'm surprised you don't know of it." There it was, a glimmer of Dotty. Judgmental, fragile Dotty.

"Dotty, thank you again for letting me come in and for having some tea and toast with me. I was famished. It's just that no one has seen you and your doctor, and well, now I too am worried about you. You just aren't yourself. You are pale and you've retreated in some ways. That's never good, at least in my experience. Is there something weighing heavily on your mind?"

Dotty was staring into the hallway. Her eyes dropped. "It's too big. I, I just can't."

"Well I hope you know that as a public health nurse, I am governed by many principles, and a pretty central one is confidentiality. Unless, of course, we know that someone is going to harm themselves or another."

"Well, that's not an issue. Except maybe I wouldn't mind hurting that slippery Bart Bignell, bilking good money out of dough heads who are way too trusting. —Just kidding. Sorta."

"Okay, well that's good. About you I mean, not Mr. Bignell." Kick paused for a few moments and then continued. "You know Dotty, sometimes when we have held onto something for so long, it seems impossible that anyone would ever understand it or that we'd be able to keep it together if we let it all out. Maybe you and I just focus on making sure that you are physically stronger, at least for now. Can we talk about how you are sleeping? Have you lost your appetite?"

"I sleep okay; at first I didn't, but it's better now. My appetite isn't very good."

"Do you think you might agree to just see your doctor so she can assess you?"

"Yes, I know she's worried. They've called a few times. Sure."

"And would you permit me to be pushy and ask to come and see you tomorrow—just to appease my own worries about you? You don't have to, of course."

"Yes, that would be fine."

The two cleaned up the dishes; Dot washed, Kick dried. "That's a lovely garden you have there. Is that zucchini I see?"

"Yes, my second batch. I'm not sure what I'll do about all of it."

"Oh, how I love zucchini bread. I have a recipe from my first preceptor when I became a public health nurse. In fact, I have probably twenty of her recipes."

"Well then, please take one. Take two! Come on, you can choose the ones you want."

After selecting some zucchini, Dotty and Kick walked back from the garden, with Kick reaching up to close her car's trunk, still chatting about how to keep Japanese beetles from eating squash. It was at this moment, when Kick's hand was in the air, waiting until Dot moved out of the way so she could close the trunk, that her reluctant patient began to share. There was something about door handles of any sort that somehow gave way to the second movement of a home visit. When many a public health nurse thinks a visit is done, after it has had its typical intro, content, and wrap-up, and the nurse has just touched the door handle to leave a house, this is the moment many patients begin to share more candidly. Maybe it takes that long to earn trust. Maybe it's about connection. Maybe it's both.

Dot looked down at the ground and cleared her throat. "Did you read the paper? The part about the Prime Minister apologizing about Canada's involvement in British Home Children?"

"Yes, I've been following that for a few years now," the socially engaged nurse replied.

"What are your thoughts about that, I mean about those kids?"

Tread lightly, the rural nurse thought. Known as "testing the waters," this sort of a conversational entrée could either move a nurse-patient relationship forward or shut it closed tight.

"Oh my. There's so much to say. But Dotty, what do you think about all of it?" Rather than unknowingly responding in an unhelpful manner, Kick shifted the conversation back to the lens of her patient. This was an important topic for Dot for some reason, and the focus needed to stay on the perspective of the patient. Not of her nurse.

Dotty winced. "They were treated like chattel. Some died. Some starved. Some were abused. Others were lucky, like … It was a different time then. So much pain and heartache." Dotty started to cry.

Kick gently moved Dotty to the side and closed her car trunk. "Let's go inside, Dot. Please." They had just made it to the front porch when the sharp-angled and shrouded older woman burst into tears.

"Sometimes I can still smell the room where we all were when we had to label our luggage. We had to make our own travelling boxes and label them. The older kids helped the younger kids, like me. The boat trip was excruciatingly long, and I remember crying until I fell asleep. Other kids vomited the entire time; it was so grueling for children that Barnardo's hired a nurse and doctor to accompany children on these sea voyages.

"My boat landed in Montreal; others went to Halifax or Quebec City. Most of the kids' names were called and they were taken to the train station for their voyage to various receiving homes. My receiving home was in Peterborough. I made some good friends there, over those six weeks. I remember being friends with two brothers; a farmer picked them out by pointing to them and saying, 'Those two will do.' He never spoke to them in the receiving parlor and when I looked out the window, he'd pushed them both to the back of his pickup truck.

"My family was a husband and wife who had no children of their own. They came in and we were all lined up. I remember thinking the woman had nice eyes and her blond hair looked soft, like my mams. She chose me and took me to live in Caledon. I only had a few minutes to pack my trunk and say goodbye to my roommates. I wish I wrote their names down, but I was too young and too afraid to ask for a pencil and paper. I wonder where they ended up and if they remained 'unwanted,' like some kids had stenciled on their trunks.

"That night, on the farm, Mrs. Pinkney gave me a bath, a new nightgown, and a teddy bear. Even though she was so kind, I was so distraught and disoriented, I could barely speak. 'Now,' she'd say. 'Tell me your full name, child. What do they call you?' Every time I tried to tell her my full name, Dorothy-Claire Langdon, I could only get out Dorothy, and only through a sob. Over and over that first night she tried, eventually both of us falling asleep. Me, in my pink canopy bed, and her in the white rocker beside it. I guess through the sobs it sounded like Dotty, and so it stuck. Since then, everyone's called me Dotty."

"That's not your name?"

"My mother called me Dorothy-Claire after both my grandmothers. I went by Claire."

"Dot, you poor thing. Thank you for telling me a bit of what's on your mind. Can you say a bit more about what it was in the paper that has you so horribly upset?"

Suddenly, Dotty got up. "I'll be right back."

After a few minutes, Dot returned. She opened her front door and looked down her lane before coming back in. She closed the screen door and main door, stating "There's a lot of nosy parkers out there." Kick heard furniture moving, and some grunting, but hesitated getting up and entering perhaps a very private room her patient would rather not be seen. Dot pushed and pushed. She pushed an old trunk from a dusty corner of a closet, through a closed off 2nd kitchen and into the kitchen as far as she could. And once this trunk became visible to her nurse, she stopped pushing.

In front of Kick was the source of decades of shame. Of self-hatred. Of pain. A one-by-two pine box with tongue-in-groove construction and stenciled lettering.

> D.C. Langdon,
> GTR (Grand Trunk Railway), No. 21,
> c/o Miss MacFinney, Peterborough, Ontario, Canada

With all the planning and preparation for home visits, one can never fully predict what will be discussed or learned. And this hidden history of a village matriarch who married into one of the hamlet's founding families is one such example. Dotty Pinkney has a secret: she doesn't really belong.

As the Paisley • Corners substitute postmistress, she spends her days telling people all the negative things about everyone else in the village. She's sure Malcolm and his "intellectually disabled" brother Ambrose are dirt poor and that they are just too prideful to tell anyone. She thinks Goody Flannigan, the school principal with her roots in Marysville, Newfoundland, killed her drunken husband and is hiding here, pretending she's something she's not. She can't understand why Olive Patterson's husband Cormack hasn't had an affair yet. "I sure as hell would," she'd say, "If my spouse was getting senile and incontinent." And she has made it her life mission to rid Paisley • Corners of Old Joe, because he's an eyesore and an embarrassment. But Dotty Pinkney, in her dry-cleaned and starched-to-perfection post office smock, is hiding the truth. It is she who knows more than anyone else the feeling of not belonging. Dotty Pinkney is a home child, sent over from England during the war—a move that forever severed any sense of home, or roots, or lineage: three things she believes defines the best sorts of families.

Kick felt gutted with what was in front of her. An exposed and motherless home child. Empathy turned to sympathy. So much about Dotty now made sense. She gently lifted Dot's chin so as to look into her swollen red eyes. "You are not your history, Dot. Our history shapes us, but it does not define us. There is no shame, except of those who abused and neglected children sent to Canada for safekeeping. That was a crazy time, a fear-infused, panicked time, when parents and grandparents were left with little choice. The government told families to do this. Maybe, I mean, well, I don't know of course. But could it be possible that this decision was in some way the highest form of love and self-sacrifice your family could give at the time? In a bid to protect you and ensure you had a future, your mother sent you on that boat. Barnardo's reassured parents in the papers and on the radio. From what I read, England was bombed terribly, over and over and over."

Shaking her head in disbelief in what she was hearing, Dotty sat up, just a little straighter. "How do you know so much about this?"

"I went to a presentation by the founder of the British Home Child Association. That's the group that convinced the Canadian government to apologize. They work now to link people back to the UK—to re-establish lost ties. They do amazing work; many of their members were home children themselves or their descendants."

"That—that sounds interesting," Dot conceded.

Dot was exhausted and Kick knew it. "You look so tired, Dot. Maybe I need to let you rest. Would that work for you? I can come back tomorrow and can bring you that information."

"Yes, I'm tired. But Kick, you won't tell anyone, will you?" Dot asked, her eyes pleading.

"No, I will not. Do you have anything you can eat later—for dinner I mean?"

"Yes, nurse, I will eat." The two got up, arranged themselves and their clothing neatly, saying nothing more of substance. Nothing more was needed. Dot half smiled and waved as Kick got into her car and began to back out of her lane.

Kick waved back. *Nursing is a privilege*, Kick thought. *A humbling, life-altering privilege.*

It didn't take Old Joe that long to pack up his belongings. He didn't have much. What took time, making him feel more and more panicked, was all the effort to try to remove any evidence that he had been there. He feared he'd be jailed for making an "illegal encampment," as the paper called them.

He loves this place. The birds, the wildlife. The frogs. He chose it after several other locations because of its morning warmth and the access to a spring that none of today's kids know about, one that isn't visible from any vantage point. The spot is far enough away, yet close enough for him to drop off wood to the Putney's back door, walk along the Caledon Trailway during downtimes, and go to Foodville in the dark of night.

"Where am I going to go?" he muttered to himself as he packed up his things in two mesh feedbags. Who wouldn't give him away? he wondered. *Ambrose. That's it! The Putney place.*

Joe made his way to the farthest end of the Putney farm to the vacant fifth wheel trailer, where Malcolm used to live when Loretta lived with Ambrose in the farm's main house. Joe knew it was a risk to go in there, but what choice did he have? He figured he would stay there for a day and try to figure out just what to do. The thought of going to Toronto scared him. He didn't want workers providing him services. He didn't' want to go into a shelter—he'd heard of theft from desperately poor people. And if he left, he wouldn't be able to find ways to give back to Paisley • Corners for all the years he'd been allowed to stay there, albeit unenthusiastically.

Malcolm was out mending a few farm posts when, out of the corner of his eye, he saw Old Joe carrying what looked like … feed bags? Malcolm watched him trying hard to not let Joe know it. He'd gotten good at it, for he knew Old Joe didn't really want anyone to look at him—to see him. He watched Joe get closer and closer to the old fifth wheel and then enter through the unlocked door.

Malcolm stopped what he was doing and rubbed his chin, letting it sink in. Glad, he felt. Now Joe would have his own place. Gathering his tools, Malcolm muttered, "Why didn't I think of this before?" and made his way home to put dinner on and tell Ambrose the news.

CHAPTER TEN
SHE WANTED SOCKS

With a one-knuckled tap, Tanis entered Jo Fraser's room, clipboard in hand. "I'm here to do your pre-op admission," she said, pulling the bed curtains aside and glancing at the clock.

Recognizing the Foodville checkout girl, Jo smiled.

It had been a very busy week for Jo Fraser, preparing not only for her hospital admission, but also trying to tie up loose ends, knowing she'd be out of commission for a while. Her fifty-fifth anniversary of graduating from the Mack School of Nursing was coming up that fall, and she'd been asked to give a speech. Every morning and every night, Jo worked on the speech, trying to decide what elements she wanted to bring forward. "Dignity, duty, diligence." Yes, that was right. And staying true to the core elements of the profession while being nimble enough to grow with societal change was key. Blending the old with the new and being open to both.

This, to her, was also the answer to the battles still percolating back home in Paisley • Corners. Embracing the 'old' while welcoming in change. More than fifty years, and much had changed except for what she understood the nurse's role to be. She just *had* to get it right, this speech. So much hinged upon it, she felt. To embrace what was while maintaining an open door to future iterations of her chosen profession — this was the balance she sought in her planned reflections. Packing her overnight bag and tucking in the speech to work on at the hospital, she reviewed her to-do list. Nearly everything was checked off. See lawyer/finalize will: done. Neighbour to water the garden: done. Cancel hair appointments: done. Secure two-week stay at rehab centre: done. Drop off two large casseroles and hand-knit gloves and hats to the Putney Farm: done. She was ready.

"I finished all the forms; they're there on my bedside table," Jo told her student nurse.

"Any allergies? Any adverse reactions to anesthetic? Roll up your sleeve, please."

"My dear, shall we start with the basics?" Jo twisted her hospital-issued name band to show her name and birthdate.

"Your blood pressure is a little elevated. You should limit your salt intake, at your age." Tanis entered Jo's vital signs on the flow sheet hanging from the end of the bed and replicated this charting in two other requisite areas. Standing up, she smoothed her university-mandated smock. The student nurse closed the interaction by stating, "The anesthetist will be in soon with the consent forms. Any questions for me?"

"Yes, actually. What semester are you in—is this your final placement?"

"Yup. I'll be applying to the *Emerg* department at Mount Sinai in Toronto. They see a lot of action there."

"Miss Eccles, you may take your break now," a friendly voice called from just outside the door.

"Ugh, that's my clinical instructor."

"Take all you can from every experience my dear. You never know what you'll need over this wonderful career of ours."

Tanis smiled. "Thanks. I'll be back after my break."

Tanis met others from her clinical group in the cafeteria for break. "Who has Mr. Gratton today?" Brandon, one of the student nurses asked the group.

"I had him yesterday. Thank God not today. What a stench," Tanis lamented.

"What do you mean?"

"I mean his feet. Gawd. How hard would it have been for him to follow his diabetic diet? It's his own fault he's losing his leg. He probably had years of warnings," Tanis responded.

"I'm not so sure about that," Brandon replied. "We have to think about options for people. Not everyone has access to non-processed foods or foods that are considered healthy but are also affordable. Also, maybe he has a history of trauma. I mean, we know that trauma robs people of the motivation needed for self-care. We don't know everyone's stories. I'm not sure it helps to blame people … just meet them where they are at and try to remove barriers they might face. That's what I try to do, anyway."

Usually quiet, Adina took a sip of her coffee, listening to the discussion unfolding amongst her peers.

"I hear what both of you are saying," Adina said, wading into the debate. "I remember our community health professor criticizing what she called 'the choice discourse.' 'Look for what's getting in the way,' she'd say. I just love that. She taught us to 'think upstream' and 'look beyond the bedrails.' She's why I want to go into public health when I graduate. I'd love to work with a community and clients and advocate to make the healthier choice ... the easier choice."

The rest of the group drank their coffee and checked their phones. After a period of silence, Tanis responded, somewhat dejectedly. "I'm just saying I couldn't stand another day with that smell in the room."

Tanis wasn't having the best experience during her nursing consolidation: the time when nursing students have a three-month, final supervised clinical practicum in order to integrate all their skills and ready themselves for an entry-level position after passing national exams. She felt her clinical instructor was "riding her" and unfairly suggesting her therapeutic relationship skills were lacking. Just the other day, on her commute to her placement, she complained about it again to her best friend over the phone. "I mean, who fails clinical right at the end because they don't make chit chat with their patients? I'm thinking about bigger things. Like O2 saturation, muffled heart sounds, sepsis. Isn't that my job—to care for my patient's medical condition?"

"What are you going to do?" her friend asked.

"I have this extra assignment where I need to analyze an interaction between me and a patient, which is just *soooo* first year. But I'm just going to play along, do this stupid assignment, and keep my eye on my goals. *My* goals."

After break was over, Tanis returned to the nursing station, sat down, and grabbed her charting. It was going to be a long day and it was only the second twelve-hour shift of three in a row. She was going to pace herself. She pulled out her notes of meds and other timed nursing tasks for the day to see what needed doing. Her charting would have to wait. She needed to wash and shave a pre-op hysterectomy patient, do vitals on two post-op patients, and check in on her pre-op hip replacement patient for meds and vitals.

"You look glum," Jo told Tanis when she returned to the older woman's room.

Tanis shrugged. "I'm okay."

"Do you want to talk about it?"

Tanis looked out the door and down the corridor for any sign of her clinical teacher.

"It's just my clinical teacher. She's riding me. I mean, I got As in all my theory courses—I just don't get it."

"What did she identify as needing some support?" Jo asked, gently.

"I wish she worded it like that. She said I have no empathy. That I rush with patients. That I'm task focused. That I'm—" and here Tanis used air quotes— "matter-of-fact at best, whatever that means." The student nurse grimaced. "She says I'm failing that entry to practice competency. You see, there's several competencies—probably very different from when you graduated."

Little did Tanis know that Jo had been a preceptor and a clinical instructor several times over the span of her career and knew quite well, the categories of entry-to-practice competencies. She knew well that nursing was grounded in accountability, evidenced-based knowledge, ethical principles concerning safe and competent care, and relationship. Though long retired, Jo kept up.

Tanis and Jo went over the forms again, discussing any conditions and medications Jo was taking, so Tanis could report this to the surgeon and anesthetist. Jo continued to ask questions of Tanis about her life, her goals, and why she went into nursing. She tried to find a personal connection that would invoke professional empathy in the young woman.

"I wanted to be a nurse after my grandpa got sick and died at home. Watching those nurses, in the emergency department when we rushed him there once, or back home in Caledon, when he was terminal. Seeing how they interacted with him, I just knew this was for me."

"Think about how your grandpa was *treated*, Tanis. You just told me you loved seeing how the nurses interacted with him and that from a very young age, you wanted to do that also. How did they treat your grandpa, Tanis?"

Tanis thought about this for a moment. "Like he mattered. They never rushed him. They didn't talk down to him. They spoke to him while they did what they needed to do, even when they needed to change his port." Tanis stopped.

Jo smiled. "What is it dear?"

"I, uh, I'm remembering back to that time. I can see the room, the nurse, my grandpa. They treated him like you're treating me, sort of. I mean, I'm still getting things done, but we are talking."

"Yes, yes we are. And you've been so good to me. Do you see how it is different from when you first came in? Does it feel different to you?"

"I can't quite pinpoint it, but yes. It does. I felt supported by you. Like I didn't have to prove anything to you. I didn't have to show you everything I knew."

"Right. I mean, as nurses, we *do* need to know much, and we need to keep up to date in our knowledge base. It's part of our professional responsibility. In so doing we are fulfilling our sacred and self-regulated service to the public. In being reflective, as you are right this moment, we are fulfilling our accountability to self and our patients. It's part of being an ethical practitioner. Getting feedback is so difficult. I remember. I should tell you a story—But I wouldn't want to bore you. It's from the Neanderthal time and all."

Tanis glanced over to one side. "Ya, sorry about that jab about your age ... I wish you *would* tell me. I mean, any help I can get, I'd appreciate it. Especially like this. Through sharing your experiences. Stories are great."

So Jo began to share with her a story she'd never forgotten, but hadn't told anyone else. She had written it in the form of a poem, sort of, thinking she might share it as part of her speech at her nursing reunion. "Ok, here goes. It's sort of a poem. I'm supposed to speak at a nursing school reunion and this is one of my scribblings. It's not very good, but maybe there's something in there that you can take away from it."

Head of her class, first choice in hospital and unit, it was day one.

IVs beeping, used gloves streaked with blood in the garbage.

7 am report. Lewis. 11 years old. End stage. Morphine pump.

Taking notes, the face of every teacher she ever had flashed through her mind.

Everyone got up. Everyone but Josephine Fraser. Fear had anesthetized her.

Jo Fraser explained this painful experience to her student nurse, hoping Tanis would loosen the self-expectations of perfection she'd accepted. She told her that even though she'd done well, self-doubt crept in rendering her mute. Stuck. In need of support and help.

"Oh Miss Fraser. I can sooo relate. It's like, no one wants to ever show their weaknesses."

"I simply could not move. I was so afraid I'd make a mistake. A little boy, so ill, on a respiratory suppressant. I needed my preceptor in that moment to pull me back to reality—to walk me into his room. To prop me up so I could be the nurse I was trained to be. We all make mistakes, my dear. We all need a little help now and again. There's no shame in that."

"I want to be a good nurse, not just task-minded like she says I am. But I don't want to get penalized for coming forward, especially this late in the program. I guess I didn't realize, about my interactions I mean …

"Now before we get too far off track, here is your antibiotic. You did start this yesterday, I hope? You need this to prevent infection for such a large orthopedic surgery."

"Yes, I did. Thank you. I've been so busy, getting everything ready, but I did remember it. You know that speech I'm supposed to give at my class reunion; we're celebrating the fifty-fifth anniversary of getting our caps. I want to talk about what we learned, about nursing as a career, all in ten minutes or so and make it meaningful. I brought it to work on tonight."

"Wow, fifty-five years. Amazing! And me, just at the start. Well, at least I hope so."

"It's a wonderful time to be a nurse. There's been so many changes that increase our ability to practice to our full scope, while at the same time, the educational requirements continue to grow and broaden. Recently, I read in the Canadian Nurses' Association Newsletter that Canadian universities were going to ensure that in every BScN program, there'd be Indigenous knowledges infused into the basic curriculum along with a focus on the social determinants of health. Did I get that right?"

"Yes, that is right. In my program, there's a big focus on social justice, while at the same time on safety and competence. I've done really well, at least until now. If I don't pass my consolidation, I have to take it all over again and not graduate with my friends."

"Well, let's talk it through. Okay. First, one thing I learned was that talking *to* people is different from talking *with* people. It's the difference between nurse as expert and nurse as facilitator, guide, mentor. We can fill our back pocket with all the knowledge in the world and come in imparting it all to others. In many ways, this is fulfilling our own need to be needed—to be seen as smart or capable."

"Well, aren't we supposed to be and do all those things?"

"Yes, it's true, Tanis. You are so correct. That is a real strength of yours, isn't it? You are knowledgeable, you know how to find the information you need, and you memorize it after you learn it. You are generous in wanting to give it to your patients. But what if they already know a lot? What if they're not ready to hear things? What if you paused. Waited. Waded in?" Here, Jo explained herself at a slow, deliberate pace. "And what if the main goal of every Interaction was to build connection so that you *could* impart the knowledge that you both agreed was necessary? It's just shifting the order of things."

"Oh, so chit chat, then teach?"

"Well … sort of. To me, chit chat is superficial. It's almost another required task type of thing, versus authentic discussion where the nurse offers a bit of themselves through making time to talk and to listen. Truly listen. When a nurse engages in meaningful discussion with their patient, it is with the hope of making a connection that, in some small way, benefits our patient. Relationship is central, if not our core tool." Tanis listened, intently.

"It's not up to our patients to trust us. It's up to us to earn it. And this is ongoing endeavour."

"Should I tell you another story, or have I bored you to tears?"

"Yes, please! That is, if you have the time," Tanis asked.

"I remember when I was a volunteer nurse working on a mobile health unit that provided outreach nursing to street-involved persons. One afternoon, a woman came on the bus wearing men's running shoes that were torn and nearly falling off. She was limping. She was red. Her skin was flaking. Her sclera was yellow. Her nailbeds showed signs of chronic heart failure. She had pitting edema in her legs. Her neck girth was concerning. Her forearms had scratches. Of course, my mind was racing with any number of medical issues she might be facing, and I was beginning to think about what I'd teach her and where I'd refer her. But I hadn't even had a conversation with her. I had no idea, now that I think about it, what *her* priorities were.

"So I slowed myself down. Rather than launching into my assessment, I gave her a bit of time, letting her get the lay of the land, so to speak, as she was needing to look around and size us nurses up. *Could she trust us*, I imagine she was wondering? Slowing down was an intentional strategy so I could actually be with her and truly hear her. I asked her how she was feeling and was there anything in particular that we could do for her. She didn't know and looked away, adjusting her ill-fitting shoes.

"Do you have any socks?" she asked me.

I replied "yes, of course," and smiled. She chose from the basket of new socks we had and began to try to get the shoes off. She let out a cry of pain, and said, 'I think they're stuck.' My heart sank. It was twenty-nine degrees Celsius, August, and her leather runners were stuck to her feet.

"Do you want me to help?" I offered. I said, 'We can go really slowly and together we can get them off.' She agreed and I can tell you that the next hour shall last as one of most memorable interactions in my nursing career. For in that hour of kneeling before a disheveled woman, someone's possibly-forgotten daughter or mother or partner, I connected again to the true essence of nursing: empathy. All that I had assessed in her, well, it was still there. But in focusing on what she needed from me, I met her where she was at."

"How did you get those shoes off?" Tanis asked.

Jo shook her head, remembering. "Well, it wasn't easy. I soaked each foot, running shoe on, in a large bin of water. Then, with her leading, we removed the running shoes one by one. I changed the water, re-washed her feet and applied antibiotic cream and non-stick bandaging. Still on my knees. Still as her nurse for that hour and a half on an August Sunday in Toronto. I made sure to engage her in conversation, instead of focusing on the air of infection that rose up between us. Her dignity was my nursing task. She wanted socks. And as her nurse, that is what I gave her."

Tanis was quiet, pensive, affected. Jo knew to leave her in her thoughts. Such silences often feel longer than they really are. But Tanis needed it.

Jo had given Tanis the background and the courage to change how she interacted with patients. Tanis didn't feel flawed. She felt mentored.

Just then, the ward clerk buzzed into the room.

"Student Nurse Eccles, you're wanted in Room Thirty-Two. Are you able to go, or should I get someone else?"

"No, I can go. Thank you, Marcie."

Jo gave her a few last words of advice. "Now, remember. Being a great nurse doesn't require high tech. And also, you don't need to be perfect. Yes, strive to be safe, competent and informed, but don't lead with that. Lead with your interest in the person in front of you. Make the connection. They'll all be different, these connections with your patients, but I can assure you, if you lead with that, and set the atmosphere to be one of mutual respect and interest in the other, you'll enjoy this wonderful profession all the more."

"Thank you so much, Miss Fraser. And good luck tomorrow with your surgery. I'll see you in two days."

"Get some rest, dear. I'll see you later. I'm starting to feel very tired and rather anxious which is not like me. Maybe it's about the surgery, or maybe it's about me being the big shot speaker at my upcoming reunion. Would it be ok if I read you my speech on your night shift so you could help me to bring it into this millenium?"

"It's a deal."

Tanis' preceptor Anneke was always early for shift. Her dad had taught her to always get to work about thirty minutes before she needed to, so she could relax, read the paper, and ease into her day. She tried to follow his advice.

Today, she ran into a colleague, Jess, whose uniform was soiled with blood. "Jess, what happened?" the preceptor asked her friend.

Jess shook her head, her far away eyes exposed her dismay. "It's the hip replacement in Room Thirty. Miss Fraser. She blew an embolism. When I came on shift, she was increasingly anxious. Through the evening, her vitals were through the roof, and she was diaphoretic, tachycardic and tachypneic. Around two a.m., she buzzed and told me she'd had a sudden sharp chest pain, and it was getting worse. I called for back-up, repositioned her and got her on oxygen. She coughed up pink foamy mucus first, and then blood. She coded at three a.m. It was awful. I tried. We all.... We all tried to save her." Anneke hugged her colleague, pausing for a moment of shared experience. Anneke, too, had connected with Miss Fraser. Everyone who met her during her short stay on the unit just loved her and admired that she was an old school nurse with contemporary views. Jess reached into her pocket and pulled out several sheets of lined paper. "She asked me to give this to her student nurse—I think she's assigned to you, right?"

"Yes. Tanis. Did she say why?"

"No, she was getting really anxious by that point. Miss Fraser just said, she'd know what it was."

Anneke took the papers and hugged her colleague one more time. "I'm sure you did all you could. You know these things come on fast. I'll get this to Tanis this morning."

"She was so kind, Miss Fraser was. Everyone on the unit had talked about how good a conversationalist she was. That she seemed interested in everyone."

"I know Tanis spent a lot of time with her yesterday. This will be rough for her, but a good learning experience. I better go. I want to lessen her patient assignment today and make sure I have time to support her."

Just then, the unit doors swung open, and Tanis entered with two large Tim's coffees in a tray in her left hand, and her cell phone in her right. She looked up from her phone and smiled at her preceptor. A warm and authentic smile.

A final practicum experience should change the student nurse. For sure, this one would.

CHAPTER ELEVEN
IN THE GLOAMING

Come, for the dusk is our own; let us fare forth together,
With a quiet delight in our hearts for the ripe, still, autumn weather,
Through the rustling valley and wood and over the crisping meadow,
Under a high-sprung sky, winnowed of mist and shadow.

Sharp is the frosty air, and through the far hill-gaps showing
Lucent sunset lakes of crocus and green are glowing;
'Tis the hour to walk at will in a wayward, unfettered roaming,
Caring for naught save the charm, elusive and swift, of the gloaming.

- L.M. Montgomery, "November Evening"

Kick didn't often work during dusk, as this is sacred time for many
a rural farm family. A time of rest and reflection. A time just after
the best light for chores shifts to the time that animals are gathered,
machinery is turned off and mental notes of the next day's tasks
assemble. She learned this early when first arriving in Caledon as a
Public Health Nurse. But today, her visits ended later than usual, in
the gloaming time—the time when hues of blueish grey soundlessly
replace the daylight. The time when busy farm families rest, regroup,
and plan. The time when fireflies, crickets and evening birds add to
the serenity of a Caledon day's end.

It had been an odd day in other respects as well, not just in ending
later than usual. With the passing of Jo Fraser, the energy surrounding Paisley • Corners diminished. The folks there were somehow

collectively less. Chatter at the post office lessened, gossip at Bobby's Pin seemed irrelevant, and young Jamie Munsie was often caught looking far away at the one stop light in town. The streets were so quiet that the recess bell became audible, as Goody Flannigan quietly acknowledged each child that passed her by. Kick's visits today had been quieter, too, mostly focused on the health-related reasons for the visit. Some of her clients had cancelled, leaving Kick with much-needed gaps to be used for paperwork and follow up phone calls.

With her final visit complete, unlocking the door of her car, Kick glanced up to the lace-curtained window as she often did, hoping to make a connection with the seemingly shut-in recluse. Today, the familiar hand paused. With a near indiscernible wave, the elderly hand slowly retreated, this time without shifting the curtains to cover the gap.

With strict instructions for no funeral, the village was left to grieve Jo in the spaces between their comings and their goings—between the harvest and the rains. Soon, it was announced that she'd left a will which would be read by a representative of Gladley and Koning, LLC after church this Sunday at the vacant Fraser house.

No one had noticed that they'd not seen Old Joe in the village recently, and today no one noticed when he slipped into the back of the property either. The lawyer was reading aloud the will, with the list of items left to people now being provided.

"To *Dotty Pinkney*, I leave you my Samsonite luggage. May you use it when you are ready."

"To *Tanis Eccles*, my checkout girl at Foodville, now studying to be a nurse. I wish I got to know you a bit more. I really wanted to find out how nursing school was today, but I never made the time to ask you for tea. I leave you my copy of Florence Nightingale's *Notes on Nursing*, signed by nurse leaders who I aspired to emulate. May your career, our noble profession, enable you to speak up and speak out about inequities so that *health for all* isn't a catch phrase but a core goal of every nurse's intention."

"To *Abner Wilkes*, I leave you all my tools, both inside the house and out back in the shed. Your skill in barn construction is to be admired, and your leadership to help get young Seth a new barn really represented what Paisley • Corners is all about."

"To *Seth Smythe*, I leave you my father's farm journals. In them, he itemized his planting, seeding, fertilizing and harvesting plans for forty years here in Caledon. Maybe there's something in there you can build upon with your wonderful new knowledge. For a blend of the old with the new might just help us go forward in our little hamlet, especially given the environmental crisis and climate change."

"To *Kick Cavendish*, I leave you my vintage glass doorknobs, the two you commented on when we visited. We spoke of those moments in our shared careers when we'd earned the trust of our patients. I know you'll cherish these as I cherished our talks about nursing."

Other names were read, with meticulously chosen items or messages endowed. After three quarters of an hour, the lawyer announced the final entry of the will.

"And I leave my house, my car, my garden and my seeds to my beloved childhood friend, John Charles MacDonald. I ask him to accompany me for one last trip to see the lavender trilliums, so he may set me to rest at the special spot we shared during our childhood. For these experiences with you are my most cherished. They have defined me. Without you, I would not have had the gumption to leave the village and become a nurse. And while I may have nursed many in a more formal way, your anonymous gifts of self through time have nursed the world. Charlie, I am, because we were. Our childhood, our combined decades of experiences and struggles, were not two childhoods. They were one. I'll truly miss you most of all."

"Who is she talking about?" Dotty muttered to Abner Wilkes, who was trying to balance himself on a stool too small for his bottom.

"Search me. Never heard of 'im."

Quietly, meekly and with a gentle scent of Aqua Velva, Old Joe walked up the back stairs of the summer kitchen, opening the familiarly squeaky screen door.

"Oh God, I can smell him from here," Dot grumbled.

Joe cleared his voice and tidied his hair. "The person that Josephine Fraser is talking about … that person is me. *I* am Charlie MacDonald."

Kick looked up. A smile spread across her face as she recognized his kind eyes, his slight hunch. Yes, she thought. She'd seen this man before. It was the kindly man she'd met when she and her corgi first found the farm. The man who'd left so quickly that day. She looked down at the damp tissue with which she'd wiped her eyes while hearing Jo's words read out by the lawyer. *That Jo*, she thought … *always one step ahead of all of us.*

While tea was being served, overseen (of course) by Mabel Tarbox, the lawyer made his way over to introduce himself to Mr. MacDonald.

"Thank you for coming, Mr. MacDonald. Miss Fraser would be so pleased. I wasn't sure how to find you, and here you are! She spoke of you during every meeting we had. I … I feel like I know you!" The lawyer shook his hand warmly, giving him the house keys and a neatly folded rectangle of waxed paper tied with binder twine. "Something else from Miss Fraser. Something she asked me to give you if ever I was able to locate you."

Several months passed following the hamlet's loss of Josephine Fraser. Dotty Pinkney took a bus trip sponsored by the British Home Children Association of Canada, first somberly visiting the cemetery in Toronto, then making their way northeast for lunch and a visit to the monument in Peterborough. Tanis Fraser passed her consolidation, with glowing comments from her clinical instructor about her intentional self-reflexivity and the resultant growth in her interpersonal skills. She made contact with Jo Fraser's reunion committee chair and brought Jo's speech to the reunion in St. Catharines to read on her behalf. At first, she was very nervous, feeling far out of her element. Smoothing the folds out of Jo's papers, she remembered her kind eyes when she was her student nurse. Suddenly courageous, she took a deep breath and started to read the words her cherished patient had written:

> *Fifty-five years! Is that even possible? As I look out over our ever-declining group tonight, I suppose I must concede that yes, it's true. Our bodies are starting to fail, but they still hold the muscle memory of us writing our exams, turning patients, bringing newborns to new moms. Our vision is starting to fail, but we are still able to see various patients, colleagues, or practice settings that stand out for us for one reason or another. Together, fifty-five years ago, we were provided with a solid foundation as to what nursing was meant to be and how we were to enact the role we'd chosen. It may, to some, seem like what we focused on is antiquated, or old school or irrelevant. But I see connections between what was and what now is, and I also see growth. Growth in our scope of practice, and growth in what we are now allowed, yes allowed, and expected to be concerned and vocal about.*

We see uniform changes, equipment changes, treatment changes. But we also see the social determinants of health now front and centre in undergraduate nursing curriculum. Before, we were instructed to treat all of our patients equally, where today, we are expected to identify how different patients are inequitably impacted by societal decisions and practices. Before, we were expected to know a lot about everything and to impart this knowledge to our patients. Today, we must be equally knowledgeable, but we are asked to partner with patients, starting where they are at and honoring their knowledges and practices. When we were trained, when we looked at environment, it was the patient's room, the hospital, or the patient's home or workplace. That now has broadened to include water, soil, air. Nurses across the globe are concerned about planetary global health, and that makes me so hopeful.

To me, my dear Mack Training School friends, despite the passing of five decades, a nurse's duty to be safe and competent, to protect and promote health, and to collaborate with other professionals, was and remains how we are called forth to care. Caring has been expanded to advocacy, policy, politics. Now when we see something, we speak up. We are witnesses, we are. And I'm so glad that the old way of 'Video et Taceo'—I see and I am silent—has been replaced with a sustained expectation within our national code of ethics to be vocal advocates for the health of all.

I recently spent time with a student nurse on the precipice of her career, and we had wonderful conversations about her experiences and mine. I realized that yes, we were divided by decades, but not by duty.

For regardless of the passage of time, our dedication to individuals, families, communities and our profession remains unchanged. I am convinced that the future of our profession is in capable hands. Competent hands. Courageous hands. Thank you for the honour of bringing these small reflections forward this evening.

While some people grew accustomed to "Old Joe" staying in the village and living in the Fraser house, others continued to grumble, complain, and gossip. He could be seen driving Jo's Subaru to Foodville, or to the Putneys' to lend a hand. He could be seen washing away decades of dust from the upper windows of his inherited board and batten house. He could be seen pruning, raking, shoveling. And now, rather than concealing his existence, buoyed perhaps by the love of his childhood friend, this gentle man stepped out from the ravine-dirtied shadows of manmade judgement. He welcomed visits from Kick, exploring new muffin recipes with each scheduled visit's preparations. And at the close of each visit, he provided her with an apple basket full of provisions "for some of your more needy patients." The public health nurse was so appreciative, and every time she delivered one of these anonymous gifts to her clients, she was struck anew by the profundity of this gesture from a man who had been treated so poorly, who had so little for so long, still choosing to give so much. Why, Kick thought, did it take a car, a house, an address for Old Joe ... no, Charlie to be seen? Are we defined by what we have? Is our value or lack thereof wrapped up in possessions? Our position? Our mistakes? Is what we 'see' channeled through our expectations? How can one man be viewed so differently, so contrarily? Is he not the same man before the address, the house, the car? Why did it take the death of one to enable the (re)birth of another?

To my door came grief one day
In the dawnlight ashen grey
All unwelcome entered in,
Took the seat where Joy had been …

- L.M. Montgomery, The Blythes Are Quoted

On a warm day late in the following spring, Charlie was ready. He packed a lunch and put in a can of Grape Fanta. In his cooler bag, he placed a cardboard divider on top of his sandwich and pop, then added the folded waxed paper the lawyer had given him. "Something from Jo for you," the lawyer had said. Then Charlie picked up the silver urn, cradling it in his underarm, and made his way to the car. His car. He still truly hadn't let that sink in.

He made his way to the Badlands, now with a parking area added by the town. Charlie didn't enter the Badlands there, though. He drove to a side road, parked, and walked. Just like before. Just like always.

He walked the route that he and Jo walked decades ago. He found one of their favourite jetted spots overlooking a valley. He set his cooler bag down and placed the urn beside it. Knowing what he'd been asked to do, he opened the urn. Handful by handful, Charlie said goodbye to his childhood friend. When all that was left was half a handful of ash, he paused and clutched it to his chest.

"I'm just so sorry, Jo. I didn't know how to tell you what'd happened to me. I felt I'd let you down. Forgive me, Jo. Forgive me. I just could not let you see me like this. A fallen man. So different than when we were young." Charlie held that last half handful of ashes.

He couldn't let it go. Not yet. With his other hand, he reached into his cooler bag and took out his pop. *We both loved grape Fanta*, he thought. It was especially good today. He kissed his hand and released Jo Fraser's last remains. Placing his empty pop can in his cooler he took out the waxed paper, neatly folded and tied with twine. He released the knot, opened one side and then the other. And there lain tidily was a solitary lavender trillium, lovingly dried and pressed.

EPiLOGUE
The Longer You Look

It's true that the longer you look at something, the more of the world you see in it. All of life's longings and all of life's lessons can be seen in a barn, in a village, or through the humbling experiences of a public health nurse. Every hope, wish, fear or compromise. Every adjustment, every loss, every beauty, every wound. The lessons come in whispers, enveloping us. Changing us.

That's how it is with Kick's barn and the parallel longings of the people of Paisley • Corners – the place she's come to call home. With each animal's fear giving way to trust ... with each resident's narrative being heard and affirmed, and with the remnants of a kindly man's encampment being carefully removed, shared realities appear. For in a ravine or beneath dusty barn beams ... the same core need exists.

To matter and to belong.

ABOUT THE AUTHOR

Photo by Gary Beechey

With experiences as a public health nurse, and nursing professor, Cheryl van Daalen-Smith's deep love for her work and appreciation of the privileged lessons afforded to nurses who bear witness to the lives of diverse individuals and communities are what inspired her to write *The Chronicles of Paisley • Corners*. Prior to writing the novel, her writing has largely been academic, crafting articles on girls' and women's mental health and co-editing Canada's leading public health nursing text. A lifelong enthusiast of all things Anne of Green Gables, she studies the life and writing of Lucy Maud Montgomery through her membership in the Lucy Maud Montgomery Society of Ontario.

Through continuing education offerings, she has studied at UBC's School of Creative Writing and the Humber School for Writers – two programs for which she is deeply indebted. She dedicates *The Chronicles of Paisley • Corners* to Canada's public health nurses who understand it well when she writes that 'Health is a matter of who matters.'

Cheryl lives in rural Ontario with her husband, their corgi Jack, orange tabby Finnigan and a menagerie of beloved farm animals.